Purpose Lies Within

Kimberly S. Phillips

Messenger Publishing

Purpose Lies Within

Published by:
Messenger Publishing
P.O. Box 373424
Decatur, GA 30037
web: www.messengerp.com

ISBN: 0-9667913-0-4
Library of Congress Catalog Card#: 98-92160

Printed in the USA by

MORRIS PUBLISHING

3212 East Highway 30 • Kearney, NE 68847 • 1-800-650-7888

Acknowledgements

First, I want to thank God for guiding me spritually in writing this novel. Many people have helped me along the way. I want to thank my husband for his support and my mom, dad, and brother for motivating me along the way.

Chapter #1

It was 1983 and the colorful leaves were dancing gracefully along the sidewalk. Dark storm clouds began filling the sky and the cool breezy wind caused the trees to sway from side to side.

Thirteen year old Nia Yolanda Chevez was strolling to her neighborhood. She was coming from her best friend, Charlene's house.

Her dark wavy hair was pulled into a long bushy ponytail and her luminous brown eyes reflected her youthfulness.

The neighborhood was so nice and quiet that she could actually hear her own footsteps. Gradually the suburban area of New York gave way to the loud noisy city of Brooklyn. All around her, cars were stuck in the middle of the rush hour traffic. Feeling chilly, Nia zipped up her jacket for warmth.

In the background, she could hear motorists cursing each other and blowing their horns; people were impatient and had places to go. Nia jumped when she heard sudden yelling.

A taxi driver was screaming at the driver in the car in front of him, "Move that piece of shit out of the fuckin way. You're taking too damn long!"

The driver rolled down his window, shot a bird, and yelled, "Fuck you!"

Damn, thought Nia, that seems to be all I hear in Brooklyn, people yelling and cursing each other. Why can't people just get along and be friendly like those Southern folks I see on television, she wondered.

One day, I'm going to leave New York, thought Nia; I'm going to go somewhere far away. Slowly, Nia walked as she day dreamed about what she would do with her future.

Finally, Nia reached the subway. She put her change into the slot machine and got on the train, heading towards her side of town. On the train, she saw an elderly woman holding onto her purse tightly, as if to make sure no one would have a chance to snatch it.

On the other side of the train, some teenage boys were listening to rap music on their boom boxes. They were talking so loud that Nia could hear their conversation from across the train. Suddenly, a police officer came on the train to make sure nothing bad was going down.

Nia looked out the window. The train was going so fast that everything outside was just a blur. Eventually, the train made it to the next stop; there was graffiti all over the walls and trash everywhere. There's a major difference between Charlene's side of town and my side of town, thought Nia.

On Charlene's side of town, it was much cleaner; and the apartments were so lovely, it was where successful people, like Charlene's parents, lived. Charlene's mom was an accountant, and her dad was a lawyer. Not only did both of her parents have excellent careers, they also owned a soul food restaurant. It was good to see black people like the Thompsons owning their own business.

Sometimes Nia worked there on the weekends to make a little money. If it wasn't for the job they gave her, she wouldn't have decent clothes and extra spending money. If it wasn't for the job they gave her, she wouldn't have decent clothes and extra spending money.

Suddenly, the train came to a stop and Nia got off. As she exited the subway, she looked around. The sky finally cleared up and she could see the stars shining so brightly.

All she saw were homeless people laying in filthy alleys and sidewalks. Across the street, she saw a man exchanging money for drugs from a local drug dealer. She passed the park and saw some guys shooting hoops; they all had dreams of being the next Magic Johnson.

As Nia was about to cross the street, she passed a homeless man wrapped up in a dirty blanket with a liquor bottle in his hand. When she got to the other side of the street, she looked back and saw him gulping down his booze; the high level of intoxication gradually put the man into an abysmal sleep. Nia felt truly sorry for the guy; she knew exactly where he was coming from because, not too long ago, she and her mom had been in the same situation.

Ultimately, she reached the gates that led to her building, that proclaimed, "Hooper Housing". Nia opened the door to her building and went up another flight of stairs. She took her keys out of her purse and unlocked the door. As she walked in, she noticed the lights were very dim, and she saw her mom sitting on the couch with a man.

"Mom, I'm home. I'm home, mom," said Nia sadly.

She placed her book bag on the kitchen table and saw that roaches were crawling everywhere.

Nia looked around and said again, "Mom, I'm home."

She approached her mom and saw that she had a crack pipe in her hand.

"Damn!" yelled Nia. "My mom is in here getting fuckin stoned again. Just look at her, she's all high!"

Tears filled her eyes, then gently rolled down her cheeks like a cascading waterfall.

Nia looked at her mom, and her mom looked at her. Her mother looked awful, her hair was nappy and she was skinny as a rail. The man sitting next to her looked as if he was high too; he was and filthy. Nia stared at both of them in disgust.

"Damn! Damn it, Mama, why do you always have to do this?" cried Nia.

Her mom was in her own little world; she was so high she didn't know her own daughter. Nia kneeled down on her knees and kept on crying.

"God, why do I have to go through this? This is what I always have to see and put up with!"

She wiped her tears from her eyes; she had cried so hard her eyes were red and puffy. Nia picked up her book bag and the rest of her belongings and left.

She walked in slow motion in darkness. For some strange reason, she had been hoping that somehow her mom would have changed and was not abusing drugs. It broke her heart to see her mom looking all messed up like that. She knew that her mom was screwing up her life. Tonight she realized that her mom was a drug addict and that her mom was the only person who could change her own life. Seeing this reality was what hurt Nia the most. For the first time in her life, she actually saw things as they really were, from the perspective of a mature mind.

She saw a telephone booth across the street. Of course the phone at her home was disconnected. Nia wanted to go back to the Thompson's house to spend the night.

Nia reached the telephone booth and picked up the phone. With trembling hands, she dialed the Thompson's number. The phone rung two times and Charlene answered it.

"Hello."

"Charlene, this is Nia."

"Yeah, what's up?" asked Charlene.

"Is it all right if I come back and spend the night?"

From the pain in Nia's voice, Charlene knew that something was not right at home.

"Nia, sure you can come, you know that you can stay with us," replied Charlene.

"Do you know if it's all right with your mom?"

Charlene yelled, "Mom, is it OK if Nia spends the night!"

Mrs. Thompson quickly picked up the phone.

"Nia, is everything OK?" asked Mrs. Thompson with concern.

"No, it is not. I just want to know if I can come over?"

"Why of course you can, dear."

"Thanks."

"Do you have some extra clothes?" asked Mrs. Thompson.

"Yes, I do."

"Your mom must be high again?" asked Mrs. Thompson.

"Yeah. Thanks, Mrs. Thompson."

"Nia, you know that you are and always will be like another daughter to me, so just come on back as soon as you can. It's dangerous out there."

"OK."

Mrs. Thompson's warm words made her feel good inside. Nia never had anyone in her life who actually cared about her well being. Knowing that someone cared about her brought tears to her eyes once again. Nia hung up the phone. Man, I don't know where I would be if it wasn't for theThompsons, she thought. Nia walked in darkness toward the subway and her journey back to a place she wished she could call home.

Chapter #2

It was like a dream; they were running toward one another with their arms reaching out. He was running to her and she was running to him. She was a little girl, about six years old. He had on his army uniform looking so tall, handsome, and strong. His name tag, read "Chevez". As they were just about to reach each other and he was ready to lift her into his arms, he vanished.

"Nia, Nia, Nia wake up girl! It's time to go, we got to get ready for school! Dang, girl, wake up!" Charlene was trying to wake Nia up from her deep sleep.

Nia rolled over and yawned.

"What time is it?" she asked sleepily.

"Girl, it is going on 7:30, and we need to get up out of here. We have to be at school at 8:00!"

"OK," said Nia.

"Hurry up. Don't, I have to leave your slow butt."

Slowly, Nia crawled out of the bed and went to the bathroom. She looked at herself in the mirror and wiped the cold out the corner of her eyes. She got a face cloth and began to wash her face and then brushed her teeth. Moments later, she began brushing her long, thick, wavy hair.

She couldn't get that dream off her mind. Man, wondered

Nia, would my father really have been like that? Nia's father was Mexican. As a staff sergeant in the United States Army, he had died in combat in 1970 during the Vietnam War, while her mom was pregnant with her. Gosh, deliberated Nia, I wish that I had a chance to meet him before he died.

Man, I better stop daydreaming and get myself ready for school she thought. She was getting tired of fooling with her hair so she pulled it back into a ponytail.

As soon as Nia and Charlene got dressed, they ran down the stairs. Hastily they grabbed granola bars, since they didn't have time to eat breakfast. Finally, they got on the subway, heading for school.

"So, Nia, are you gonna try out for cheerleading, or what?"

"Yeah, I think I am."

"I always wanted to be a cheerleader."

"Me too."

"Nia, wouldn't it be nice if both of us made the cheerleading squad?"

"Yeah, it would be wouldn't it," agreed Nia.

"Hopefully both of us do make it," stated Charlene.

"I hope so too. Hmmm we would really have it going on," said Nia.

"Give me a 'W', give me an 'A', ...!" cheered Charlene, spelling out Washington High School.

"Yeah, right, girlfriend, you are so silly," laughed Nia.

"When is practice, Charlene?"

"I think it starts Friday," replied Charlene.

"Really, so we have practice on that following week?" asked Nia.

"Yep."

They got off the subway and ran across the street to the school.

Meanwhile, the bell rang and they joined the crowd of students rushing into the school building.

The halls at Washington High School was so congested with students that everyone kept on bumping into one another. The student body was made up of almost every ethnic group.

Well, here I am, Nia Yolanda Chevez, at my locker she thought. I'm at locker 2107. Yes this is me. Nia opened her locker to take out her English book. I wish Charlene's locker was right next to mines, she thought. In junior high, their lockers were next to each other, and they took almost all of the same classes together; it was like they were inseparable. But, somehow, high school was totally different. Their lockers were on opposite halls, plus they took none of the same classes.

Slowly the day went by and to Nia it seemed like the day was lingering along in slow motion. Ultimately, it was time for lunch. Nia and Charlene met in the school cafeteria.

"So, girl, how are your classes so far?" asked Charlene, a grin filling her pretty chocolate colored face.

"Oh, girl, please, school is school." Nia rolled her neck.

"Nia, you need to get serious about school. You know that, don'tyou?"

"Who cares." Nia began rolling her eyes and checking out her freshly filed fingernails.

She wanted Charlene to get off the subject; she just didn't want to hear her lecture.

"I care, Nia, and I want to go to college one day."

"Well, that's you, girlfriend." Nia started eating her cheeseburger and fries.

"Don't you want to go to college?" questioned Charlene with concern.

"Yeah, maybe one day, now, I just want to get up out of here."

"You will one day Nia, but now you need to get serious about the books."

"You soundin like your mama."

"Yeah. And you know what? Mom is right."

"Well, I guess she is," uttered Nia.

"Personally, I think you should be more concerned about school because it can be your ticket out of the ghetto. Aren't you tired of the ghetto?"

"Yeah I am tired of being there, and I'm going to go somewhere, girl."

"Where are you going to go?"

"I'm gonna leave New York,"

"Yeah, but if you don't get serious about your education, you ain't going anywhere." Charlene snapped her head with an attitude.

"Oh come on Charlene, why don't you chill a little? Take a chill pill!"

"OK, Nia, I'm gonna lay off but for real you do need to take it seriously."

"I make C's."

"Yeah, and you also make D's. You need to pull up your grades."

Nia was getting very annoyed so she crossed her arms in front of her chest, and tears began to fill her eyes. What Charlene was telling her was hurting her feelings.

Charlene saw that Nia was upset so she said, "Girl, I'm not trying to hurt your feelings, I'm being a friend and just being honest with you. You need to pull up your grades if you want to get somewhere in you life."

"I am going to get somewhere, I know I am," mumbled Nia.

Nia knew that Charlene was right, but it upset her to hear her best friend telling her that she was not doing her best. She knew Charlene was not trying to hurt her, that she was trying to inspire her to do better.

After lunch, Nia went to her next class. What Charlene told her earlier had her really thinking about which direction she needed to take in school. Maybe Charlene is right, maybe I do need to be more serious about my school work, she thought.

Hell, I'm young, I am thirteen years old, and I have plenty of time to think about my future. But, then again, I want to get up out of here, she thought. I don't want to be in the ghetto for the rest of my life. I want to be somebody. I want to make it, and I am going to make it, that's one thing for sure!

After school, Nia and Charlene met up to go to the cheerleading meeting. At the meeting, they found out when and where practice and tryouts were being held. The meeting only lasted for thirty minutes.

"Nia, are you going to make it to practice tomorrow?" asked Charlene.

"Yeah, I'm not going to miss this for nothing."

"Me either, girl. I'm going to be there."

"Well, I guess we better head on home then," stated Nia.

"Home?"

"Yeah."

"Are you coming over to my house tonight, Nia?" questioned Charlene.

"Um, I'm going to stop by my house first, to see how things are going. I need to check up on my mom," answered Nia.

Charlene was about to say something but then she change her mind, so she said, "Never mind."

"No, Charlene, what was you going to say?" asked Nia.

"No, I think it's none of my business," stated Charlene, looking away.

"Girl, you are my best friend, and I want to know your opinion about things that are important in my life."

"I don't understand you," expressed Charlene, shaking her head with disapproval.

"What?"

"Your mom is up there using drugs. She doesn't know that you even exist. She could care less if you come home at night, and she doesn't even care about where you are. She doesn't give a damn about you, girl!"

Nia couldn't say a word because she knew that Charlene was right; all Nia could do was lower her head. Her heart was telling her she must go and see if her mom was OK.

Charlene continued talking.

Nia looked at her and responded, "Because she is my mom, that's why."

"Nia, she's a junky, that is what she is!"

"Come on, Charlene, that is my mom, and I care about her! I should really see how she is doing at least every once in a while."

"You know what? You should just come and stay with us always. You don't have to put up with all of that."

"I know, but I just want to see if she is OK."

"All right then, you can always come on over later," said Charlene.

"OK, thanks girl, I'll see you later," said Nia as she hugged Charlene.

"OK."

Instead of walking with Charlene to the subway station, Nia

walked on home to the projects.

On her way, Nia played a little game on the sidewalk. She tried to see how many cracks she could avoid stepping on. Moments later she stopped focusing on the cracks on the sidewalk and started to kick some of the rocks lying on the pathway. Playfully Nia kicked the rocks to see how far she could make them move along the sidewalk.

Suddenly, her playful mood left, and she began to observe the things going on around her. She looked up the street and saw some girls playing double dutch near the fire hydrant. Nia stopped for an instant and watched them jumping rope.

Nia started walking again. She put her hands in her jacket to try and keep them warm. Swiftly, a group of kids ran past her playing Hide-N-Seek. She sat down on a bench to watch. She saw a little boy, about seven years old, close his brown eyes and count while his friends ran to find hiding places.

The child yelled, "Ready or not, here I come!"

Nia smiled as she watched them play. Unexpectedly, a frown came across her face as she thought about how her childhood had been taken from her.

Across the street, Nia noticed that there were some people dealing drugs. She moved on along and saw people playing craps, gambling to rip each other off for money. Nia shook her head and wondered how people could actually be foolish enough to fall for those idiots schemes.

Up the street, she saw people break dancing. They were competing against each other to see who was the best dancer on the block. For a while, Nia stood and watched them dance. She even started to dance to the groove. The rap music was on, it was the kind of music that made people want to get up and show off all their street moves.

Nia was having fun, but she knew it was time to move on. She picked up her book bag and headed on. She passed a dirty local park with litter everywhere and graffiti on the walls. Some boys were playing basketball on the courts.

Finally, Nia reached Hooper Homes. She jogged up the flight of stairs and saw the curse words written on the dark, filthy, cracking walls. On some of the steps, there were beer cans, cigarette butts, liquor bottles, and old news paper.

Abruptly, a huge obese rat ran right in front of Nia's path; she jumped because it scared the daylights out of her and frowned when she discovered it was only a rat. Damn, this fuckin place should be condemned, she thought.

As Nia got to the top of the stairs, she saw her next-door neighbor, Fanny. Fanny sometimes hung out with her mother. She was also a drug addict; she mainly shot up heroine.

"Hi, Fanny," said Nia.

"Hi, how is it going?"

"Fine," answered Nia.

Fanny didn't look so hot. She still had rollers in her hair, her eyes had bags under them, and she had nothing on but her pink fuzzy robe.

Nia noticed Fanny appeared to be in a daze so she queried, "Are you OK?"

"Girl, I just need me a hit."

She came towards Nia and asked, "Do you have $10.00 I can borrow?"

"No, I don't," responded Nia.

"Well, don't you have any money I can borrow? I could surely use a dollar bill," she begged.

"No, I don't, Fanny. I just used my money on the subway,"

replied Nia as she took a step back.

Nia knew how drug addicts were; they would move closer to you to steal your wallet, so Nia knew to keep her distance. Nia noticed that Fanny had the shakes and Nia knew she needed a hit for a quick fix. Fanny was starting to show signs of withdrawal.

"OK, then."

"I'll see you later."

"Bye," uttered Fanny.

Nia watched her as she walked away, then turned around to unlock the door. Nia lied when she told Fanny she didn't have any money; she didn't feel like giving her dough for drugs. Drugs had destroyed Fanny and her family; not too long ago, a social worker had come and taken Fanny's children away from her because she was not taking good care of them. She was an unfit parent.

Well, here I am at my mom's house, Nia thought. She unlocked the door and walked on in. Nia laid her book bag down on the table.

"Mom, I'm home!"

Nia looked around and saw her mother.

"Oh , hi, dear. How are you doing?"

"I'm doing fine."

Nia smiled because she was so happy that her mom did not seem to be high today. She went over and gave her mom a hug. Her mom looked a little better than the last time Nia had seen her.

Her mom stepped back to take a good look at her little girl. All she could do was grin because her daughter resembled her father so much that it brought tears to her eyes. Nia looked closer at her mom and saw that she didn't look completely right; she was very skinny, and her eyes were red and had bags under them from using drugs.

Nia's mom name was Racheal. Both of them had the same honey colored skin and height, about five feet, three inches tall. Racheal was in the kitchen stirring some food in a bowl.

"What are you cooking?" asked Nia.

"Oh, I'm just fixing some tuna."

"Really?"

"Yeah."

Mom stood there with one hand on her slender hip and the other hand holding her cigarette. Nia watched her inhale and exhale. She saw the smoke from the cigarette silhouette into a gray cloud which eventually disappeared.

"So how was school today?"

"Oh, school was fine. School is school."

"Did you meet Charles, Nia?"

"No, who is Charles?"

"Oh you didn't meet him. Well he's in the living room, go say hi to him."

Nia peeked around the corner. Aw man, that's the same no good sucker she had over last time, the one she was getting stoned with, Nia speculated. Man, I don't feel like introducing myself, thought Nia. Meanwhile, Racheal walked into the living room.

"Charles, Charles, have you met my daughter?"

"No, I haven't met her," he replied, bored. Racheal was beaming.

"Well here she is. This is my little girl, Nia."

She spun around and saw Nia still standing in the kitchen peeking around the corner. Looking angrily at Nia, Racheal shoved her over to where Charles was standing.

"Say hi to him gul, now don't you try to act all shy!" demanded Racheal.

Already Nia knew that she despised him, so she rolled her eyes at him and said, "Hi."

Charles casually eyed Nia up and down. His eyes were glued to her breasts. Nia was well developed for a thirteen year old girl, and Charles knew that too. He liked what he saw.

He stared boldly into her eyes and said, "Hi, it's nice to meet you."

"It 's nice to meet you, too," mumbled Nia as she distastefully shook his hand.

Nia felt very uncomfortable around him. She glanced at his hands; they were very big and crusty looking, just like him.

Nia saw that he had a nasty looking drip-drop jerry curl. He was overweight, mainly because of his beer belly. Yuck! He lookes and smells like a bum, she thought in disgust. His shirt was very dirty. She just couldn't understand what her mom saw in this man.

Nia walked away from both of them and turned on the T.V. to watch "The Jeffersons". Nia was crackin up over George and Florence because they kept on jonin each other. Suddenly a wave of uneasiness came over Nia; she felt someone watching her. She turned around and discovered that Charles was staring at her. Lust was all over his face. His eyes were piercing with fire, as he licked his lips. She watched his hands go down to his crotch. He began to fondle himself. Nia turned around in repulse; she knew that Charles was definitely a sick man.

She shot out of the room; his presence made her feel scared and unsafe. Charles snickered; he found the whole thing to be hilarious. That's a fine little young thang Racheal has, and one day when I am alone with her, I'm going to take advantage of her sweetness, he thought to himself. He continued to laugh out loud as he thought about the fear he saw in her eyes; he knew that she knew what he had in store for her. In his wicked train of thought, he picked up his whiskey bottle and took another sip.

Nia went to the kitchen.

"So Nia, are you going to stay here today?" Racheal asked.

Nia hesitated a little and said, "I might stay here, I don't know."

"Do you want some tuna?" asked Racheal, cutting her tuna sandwich in half. Nia looked around and saw roaches crawling everywhere, crumbs all over the counter, and dirty dishes scattered all over the kitchen.

"I don't think so Mom," she answered politely.

She had noticed that the whole place was in shambles. Nia used to try to keep the apartment clean, but by the time she finished cleaning up, her mom and her crackhead friends would have everything messed up again. She felt that there was no point in cleaning up anymore, so she just let it be. She had tried just about everything to keep the house clean.

After Racheal finished eating her tuna sandwich, she picked up her crack pipe. Nia became teary eyed; she didn't want to see her mom high again.

"Mom, do you really want to do that right now? Can't we just sit down and talk?"

With frustration in her voice, Racheal asked, "Nia, what is there to talk about?"

"We never talk like we used to. Do you remember the times we spent together, just you and me? You used to work those two jobs, and we lived in an apartment on the other side of town. Do you remember those days, Mama? I loved those days, Mama". Nia spoke fast, hoping to start a nice, long, warm conversation with her mom for a change.

Racheal was getting tired of hearing Nia talk about the good old days, because she didn't want to remember it. All she cared about was getting high and feeling good.

Angrily Racheal answered, "Yeah, I remember those days too, but do you remember when we were thrown out, evicted, and homeless?"

"Yeah, I remember that too, Mom. But, at least, we had each other. Why can't things be like they were?"

Racheal gently cupped Nia's face with her hands and responded, "Honey, time moves on, remember that. I like this drug. I need it. It's the only way I can survive."

"Mom, I'm losing you. You're not the same," cried Nia as she held her mom's hands.

"Darling, it might not ever be the same."

Racheal lit a match and inhaled the smoke from her pipe. Racheal was gone, gone off into her own little world. And Charles was still sitting on the couch drinking his liquor. He, too, was intoxicated into his own little world.

Nia wept. Her own mom didn't want to sit down and have a mother and daughter talk with her. Man, my own mom never even told me about the birds and the bees, Nia thought. Mrs. Thompson was the one who spoke to me about sex, she thought. Every time she went home, she always ended up disappointed and depressed; it seemed like her mom was pushing her away and didn't want to be bothered with her. Shit, maybe Charlene was right about my mother, thought Nia, it just seem like she does not give a damn about me.

Nia picked up her book bag and made preparations to go to Charlene's house. She might as well call the Thompsons her family; she felt more at home at their house than she did at her own. It was a tragic feeling to know that she was losing her mom to drugs, but this was the harsh reality she had to deal with.

She got her stuff out of her room. Then she walked to the subway station, put her money into the slot machine, and headed on her way. She had made up her mind that she was not going over to her mom's house anymore. Besides, she thought, my mom has Mrs. Thompson's phone number so she knows how to reach me; Nia was finally weary of her mom and had decided to accept things as they were and get on with her life without her mom.

She reached the Thompsons' and rung the doorbell. Mrs. Thompson opened the door with a smile and a hug. Mrs. Thompson was happy to see Nia and just wished that she could adopt her and really make her a solid part of their family.

Nia was about to ask her if she could stay over when Mrs. Thompson interrupted her saying, "Girl you come right on in here!" She opened the door wide to let Nia in. "You don't have to ask me just come right on in, you're a part of this family."

"Thanks," smiled Nia.

Nia went upstairs to Charlene's room. Nia put her things down on the twin size bed and went back downstairs. She washed her hands and went into the kitchen to help Mrs. Thompson chop up lettuce for the salad.

"So, how was it seeing your mama?" asked Mrs. Thompson.

"It was OK," replied Nia with lack of enthusiasm.

"Is she still using that stuff?"

"Yeah, but at least this time she was not high when I first saw her."

"That's good. Did you get a chance to talk to her for a while?"

"Yeah a little bit, for a little while. She had this man over, and I don't like him," frowned Nia as she thought of Charles.

"Yeah, don't she always do," added Mrs. Thompson, rolling

her eyes.

"I'm glad you let me stay over here, Mrs. Thompson, this is the place I can truly call home." Nia's eyes filled with love for this dear person.

"Nia, you do have a place to call home. You can call this your home. Nia, you're a good kid, you remember that," said Mrs. Thompson, tossing her salad.

Nia beamed, because she hadn't heard a good word about herself in a long time. The compliment made her feel mellow deep inside.

She always heard negative things from her mama. Mom always told her that she was nothing, that she would never amount to anything, and that she would always be nothing. Hearing this compliment from Mrs. Thompson made Nia feel stronger and more confident about herself. Nia reached over and hugged Mrs. Thompson, Mrs. Thompson hugged her back.

After she finished helping with dinner, Nia went upstairs. That night she actually sat down and did her homework. She hadn't done that in a long time; for a change, she really studied.

Chapter #3

The colorful leaves of October 1983 gave Washington High a bright background. Finally it was Friday, the day of cheerleading tryouts. Getting ready in the girls' locker room, Nia and Charlene were excited but nervous at the same time.

They reached the gym and soon, it was time for their routines. Alphabetically, Coach Williams called out the names of the girls who were trying out. Nia was one of the first to perform, because her last name started with a "C".

Abruptly, Coach called out her name.

"Nia Chevez."

Nia went to the middle of the gym floor. She did her cheers with perfection. Her heart was beating as fast as a locomotive, her stomach had butterflies, and the palms of her hands were sweaty.

Nia included flips, cartwheels, splits, and enthusiasm in her cheer. Eventually she was finished, and she stood before the judges for a brief moment which seemed like an eternity. Coach finally told her that she could sit down.

Nia felt relieved. She was proud of herself; she knew that she had given it her best shot. Charlene moved to where Nia was sitting.

"You did great," whispered Charlene.

"You really think so?"

"I know so. You did your routine perfectly. They are going to definitely choose you."

"Yeah, I hope that you are right, girlfriend."

Meanwhile, Coach had called almost everyone's name on the list. Nia noticed that Charlene was chewing her nails; whenever she got nervous about anything, she always chewed her fingernails like a squirrel nibbling on an acorn.

Finally, it was Charlene's turn. She walked to the middle of the gym floor to begin her routine.

Nia keenly observed Charlene as she did her cheers. Charlene did everything she was supposed to do. She finished her routine and Charlene had done an excellent job.

"How did I do?" questioned Charlene as she approached Nia.

"I think you did great," whispered Nia.

"Thanks. You didn't mess up, either."

"We tried our best, and that's what really counts."

After the tryouts were over, Coach Williams stood before the girls and gave a brief speech. "Well girls, all of you did a wonderful job. Now we are going to ask you to take a fifteen minute break, to get a soda or whatever snack you want and come right back. During the break, the judges will be calculating the scores and decide on who made the team."

Coach Williams walked away swiftly.

"That Coach Williams is a trip," remarked Nia with a smirk.

"Yeah, she is," agreed Charlene.

"She always have her nose up in the air, talking like she's all that!" exclaimed Nia.

"Yep," laughed Charlene.

"Hey, I'm Ms. Williams, I'm Coach Williams," said Nia, mocking Coach with her nose in the air and her hands on her hips.

"Girl, you are crazy, you are up here mocking her," laughed Charlene. Nia was imitating Coach Williams to a T.

"Yeah, but she does talk like that and have her nose way up in the air," said Nia with a silly expression on her face.

"You need to stop mocking her," added Charlene, trying to keep a straight face.

"Girl, you know that it is funny," laughed Nia.

Charlene could not hold in her laughter; she started laughing so hard that tears began to roll down her cheeks.

"Girl, you're so silly," chortled Charlene trying to catch her breath.

During their break, Nia and Charlene went downstairs to the vending machine. Nia got herself a Snickers bar and a Coke Cola, and Charlene bought herself a bag of Doritos and a Sprite. They sat at one of the tables located near the snack bar.

"All right, cross your fingers," said Charlene.

"I'm going to cross mines." Charlene was really munching on her Doritos like they were going out of style.

"Man, it would be so smooth if we get to wear those uniforms and go to every basketball game. We can really check out all those fine boys," said Charlene.

Gosh, thought Nia, Charlene can really talk fast and put so many words together in one combined sentence. Most people had to tell her to slow down, but fortunately, Nia understood every word she said.

"Girl, you are boy crazy," laughed Nia.

"You are too, Nia. You know that you look at all those guys."

"Yeah, I know." Nia couldn't deny that because she knew it

was true.

Out of the blue, a good looking guy walked down the hall. Nia looked up and saw him. Dang, home boy is fine, she thought. I need to go check him out.

"Wait a minute, did you see that boy right there?" said Nia excitedly, pointing in the direction the cute guy was walking.

"What boy?" asked Charlene.

"That boy that just—come on, lets get up and find him!" Nia reached over and playfully pulled Charlene out of her seat.

"Girl, you are crazy, why are you going to follow this guy?"

"I am following him because he is F-I-N-E, fine!"

They rushed to try to find the handsome stud.

Nia's heart was beating fast. For some reason, she knew that she had to meet this guy.

"Girlfriend, are you insane? You don't even know this guy!" exclaimed Charlene.

"And you had the nerve to call me boy-crazy! At least I'm not the one running up and down the school halls trying to find this big hunk!"

As she peeked around the corner, Nia spotted him.

"Come here, Charlene, there he is," whispered Nia. Both of them took a peek at Mr. Good Looking himself.

"Oh, that boy is fine," agreed Charlene.

"Shh, shh, he might hear us."

He stood at his locker taking out some books and putting them inside his book bag. He was very tall, perhaps six feet tall, with a medium brown complexion. He also had a cute fuzzy mustache, Nia observed. The guy had on a blue Washington High basketball jersey, black sweat pants, and a pair of black Nike basketball high tops.

"Do you know him?" asked Nia.

"No, I don't know him."

"Hmm...he must be in the ninth grade, then."

Nia wondered who he was; she rubbed her chin, plotting about how she was going to get this guy to notice her without looking like a complete fool.

"He might even be a tenth grader. Um, I wouldn't mind meeting him," admitted Nia.

"Why don't you go up to him, girl?"

"Nah, he might not like me, and I don't want to look too obvious."

"How do you know if he don't? Why don't you just say 'hi' and introduce yourself?"

"Nah, I don't think I should do that."

"Nia, you acting all shy! Just go up to the boy, he's only a human being."

"That's easy for you to say, Charlene! You can't even go up and talk to that boy name Scott you like so much because every time you see him you, drool."

"Now Nia, that's a different story," said Charlene folding her arms across her chest.

"How is that different?"

"It's different because Scott is drop dead gorgeous and super fine, and I ain't going near him."

"Girl, you know that you like Scott, and you should try to talk to him."

"What are you trying to do, Nia? Are you trying to keep yourself from approaching this guy or what?" Charlene could see right through her little scheme of trying to change the subject.

"You must be scared, Nia."

"Yeah, I'm afraid. What if he turns me down, and what if he doesn't like me?"

Nia paused for a moment. Suddenly she came up with a neat idea.

"Maybe if I walk by and smile, maybe I can get his attention."

Nia looked around the corner and noticed that home boy was walking away from his locker and starting up the steps.

"Oow, girl, we got to catch up! He's going up the steps!"

Running side-by-side, they and fled up the steps after the guy.

At the top of the staircase, the mysterious guy was talking to another boy who was also wearing a basketball jersey. They must be going to basketball practice, speculated Nia.

"Maybe if I walk on by them, he would look at me."

"You could try it."

Nia made up her mind to stroll by them. She walked on by him slowly with a casual but seductive stride; she looked at him, hoping that he would notice her. At last, he looked up and saw her. They made instant eye contact; he smiled first, and then Nia smiled back.

After she passed by them, he grinned and asked his friend Marcus, "Hey, man, did you see that cute girl that just walked past us?"

"Yeah, she's fine."

"Do you know her, man?"

"Naw, I don't think I know her, but I have seen her before. I think she's in the eighth grade."

"Man, she has a nice body for an eighth grader. Gosh, imagine how good she'll look when she gets in the eleventh or twelfth grade."

Clay turned his head as he watched Nia going down the hall and down the steps. I wonder what her name is, he wondered; I'm going to surely find out, he thought.

Nia jumped up and down when she caught up with Charlene. "He noticed me, he noticed me, he noticed me, girl!" she shouted.

"You're so silly," uttered Charlene.

Nia kept on bouncing around, "He even smiled at me, girl."

"I saw it, he smiled."

"And I smiled back. Maybe he does like me."

"Yes, he smiled but that does not mean anything. Just take it one step at a time and don't rush things."

"OK, OK, OK, but he is cute!"

"Yeah, I have to admit he is cute," smiled Charlene.

"Well, our fifteen minutes are up, and we need to go back downstairs to see if we made it," stated Charlene while glancing down at her watch.

"OK."

They ran down the steps and reached the gym. The judges were still calculating the score.

"Gosh, they're not finished yet. We could have stayed upstairs and kept on flirting."

"Girl, you are crazy," repeated Charlene.

"And you are, too," added Nia. They giggled.

"If Scott was up there you would be drooling."

"Yeah, you ain't joking about that."

"And I know that for a fact."

Moments later, Coach announced who had made the cheerleading squad.

"Well, girls, we have the list of who made the squad. For those who didn't make it, we are glad that you have least tried..."

Yeah, yeah, yeah, just call out the names, thought Nia.

Coach continued to talk, "...And we ask you do try again, because next time you might make it. For those who did make the squad, congratulations, all right then."   It's about time she stopped yapping that mouth of hers, thought Nia.

Finally, Coach Williams called out the names.

"Amy Adams." Amy was jumping up and down with joy; she was so thrilled and happy.

"Brenda Lansky."

Dang, I wish she would call out my name, Nia thought.

Coach called some more names and then some more names. Nia's stomach was filled with butterflies; she really wanted to make the team.

Finally, she heard Charlene's name .

"Charlene Thompson."

Nia reached over and hugged Charlene because she was so happy for her.

Gosh, I made it!" beamed Charlene.

The coach called out all the names except Nia's. Dang, she called everybody's name except mines, thought Nia. She sighed, thinking she hadn't made the squad. She looked down in gloom, and tears began to fill her lovely almond-shaped brown eyes.

"The last person is Nia Chevez." Nia sighed with relief; hearing her name was like music to her ears and filled her with delight.

Nia and Charlene were grateful. They hugged each other and screamed, jumping up and down. Instead of going straight home, they decided to stop by the ice cream parlor to celebrate by ordering banana splits.

They sat down and dove into the sticky sweetness. While they were eating, Scott walked in the door. Charlene looked up with shock, "Nia is that who I think it is."

Nia turned her head and nodded, "Yeah, girl, that is?"

"Charlene, he's all right, so what if he's the star football player."

"He's such a dream," said Charlene, as she stared at him from across the parlor.

Nia turned back around and saw him standing near the cash register to place his order. She still couldn't understand what Charlene thought was so great about him. Maybe it was because he was a red bone, Charlene had a thang for light skinned guys.

"Girlfriend, he looks OK. He ain't all that," Nia stated bluntly.

"Look at his caramel colored skin and those rippling muscles."

"Girl, why don't you just go up there?"

"No way, I can't do it."

"Why don't you say 'hi' or do what I did and walk by him and smile, maybe he would notice you then."

"I can't do that," whimpered Charlene, shaking her head no.

Charlene was a very pretty girl. She had lovely, smooth, rich chocolate colored skin. Her hair was jet black, shoulder length, silky in texture. She kept her hair in a mushroom type style, popular at the time. Her stunning, sparkling, brown eyes were wide with a touch of innocence. And she had soft chubby cheeks and a very cute button nose.

With her looks, Charlene could get practically any guy she wanted thought Nia. A lot of the eighth and ninth grade boys had a crush on her, but unfortunately, Charlene had a thing for older guys; she always said that older guys were more mature than the ones her age and that is why she always chased after them.

"Charlene, you are pretty, just go over there and smile."

Instantly, a very nice looking girl walked in. She was heavy chested with breasts the size of melons. Miranda, in a pair of skin tight Jordache jeans had a fair, medium brown complexion and spectacular hazel colored eyes that most girls only dream of having. She spotted Scott and walked towards his table with a very seductive smile on her face. She placed her arms around him and gave him a kiss on the cheek.

"Miranda, Miranda, why does she always have to come up and blow everything?" mumbled Charlene.

"Well, she's not called Fast Miranda for nothing," added Nia while rolling her eyes.

"You know there's a bad rumor going around school about her, and most people think she's very fast," said Nia.

"I know she's fast. She's Miss Hot Thang, look at that skimpy outfit she has on...her blouse is too low cut and shows off everything. And look at Scott, he's drooling and can't keep his eyes off her. Man, no telling what they're going to be doing tonight," uttered Charlene in disgust.

"Well, maybe you didn't need him in the first place," said Nia.

"Maybe I don't need him because I heard that he's a dog anyway!"

"Yeah, you don't need a dog, Charlene. You know, there are better guys and other fish in the sea," smiled Nia wisely.

"Yeah, you're right, girl. I just wish he knew I exist, though," moped Charlene.

"He's not going to notice an eighth grader. You know he's in the eleventh grade, and he probably only dates upper classmen.

"But Miranda is just in the 10th grade."

"Oh, yeah, but she's two years older than us and has a bad reputation. Guys tend to like those type of girls."

"Yeah, but one day," muttered Charlene, in a daze.

Eventually, they left the ice cream parlor and went home. Nia didn't even bother to go back by to tell her mom the good news. She knew her mom wouldn't care she had made the cheerleading squad. For a whole week, she has not been back home, she didn't have anything to say to her mom anymore. She felt that there was no point in going back; her real home was with the Thompsons now.

When they got home, they immediately told Mrs. Thompson the outstanding news about making the cheerleading squad.

"Girls, you all really made the team?" asked Mrs. Thompson.

"Yes, we did, Mom," answered Charlene gleefully.

"That's great! We're going to celebrate this special occasion. I'm going to take you all out to get some pizza." Mrs. Thompson hugged them both.

Nia and Charlene were very excited about going out for pizza. They didn't even mind that Charlene's little brother, Joseph, also tagged

along. It was the end of a very exciting day.

Chapter #4

The season of the year gradually changed. The brightly colored leaves gently dropped from the trees. And the trees were bare in time for winter.

Nia still didn't go by to see her mom; it had been several months since she had last seen her mother. Nia decided that today she was going to see her.

"So, Nia did you change your mind about going over to your mom's house?"

"No, Charlene, I think today I should go see her."

"Yeah, I guess I have to agree with you. You haven't been over there in a long time."

"I know I can't stay mad at my mom always."

"Yeah, girl, you can't be."

"Well, are you going to be back in time for the basketball game?"

"Yeah, I am. I'm going to walk to my mom's house, and then I'll head back to school," added Nia.

Charlene could tell that Nia had a lot on her mind, because she seemed very puzzled about something.

"Are you OK?"

"Yeah, I'm fine."

"Are you going to spend the night?"

"Yeah, I'm going to spend the night."

"OK, then I'll see you later."

"Bye."

They waved to each other and went on their separate ways.

Slowly, Nia walked over to her mom's house. Nia had on her thick overcoat, boots, and gloves. The snow was continuously falling from the sky; it was cold outside, so Nia wrapped her scarf even tighter around her neck. Her nose and ears were very cold from the brisk wind. Gosh, wouldn't it be nice to have some earmuffs right about now? she thought. Nia pulled her scarf over her mouth in an effort to keep warm.

Being a native New Yorker, Nia was pretty much accustomed to the cold weather of Brooklyn. There were a lot of people on the road, even though it was snowing. Nia cracked up when Charlene told her about how people in Georgia don't even go to school when it sleets, drizzles, or snow, even a little bit. Man, the snow down there is a joke compared to the snow we get up here, thought Nia.

She looked across the street and saw the same guy that she had seen in school a while back, the cute guy that she had followed around school with Charlene. Dang, he's so fine, I wonder what his name is, she thought. Nia watched the mystery guy stroll down the street with his friends until they could no longer be seen through the falling snow.

Nia kept on walking through the softly falling flakes. A million thoughts were crossing though her mind all at once. Finally, she reached her house and walked through the gates and up the stairs. She could hear her feet tapping on the steps as she ran up each step. The walls were still dirty and the place was still infested with rats and roaches. Nothing seemed to have changed.

Ultimately, she unlocked the door.

"Mom!" yelled Nia. There was no response.

Dang, Mom must not be home, thought Nia. I wonder where she is? She looked around to see if anyone was there, and then sat down at the kitchen table to wait. Suddenly, someone opened the door. Racheal walked in.

"Hi, Mom."

"Hi."

"I haven't seen or heard from you in a while," said Nia.

"I know."

"So, how are you doing?" asked Nia. She waited for her mom to look her way. Racheal hung up her coat and then came into the kitchen.

"I'm fine," sighed Racheal.

It took her a long time to respond to Nia's question. Nia looked at her mom and noticed immediately that one of her eyes was black!

"Who's been hitting you?" Nia cried with deep concern.

Nia went to the refrigerator and got some ice to put in a plastic bag.

Racheal said, "Oh, nobody." She looked away and then looked back at her daughter.

"What's going on Mom? I haven't heard from you in a while and now, this..."

Nia approached her mother and placed the ice bag on her eye. She could see that her mom was nervous and scared about something. She wouldn't look Nia straight in the face.

"I can't call you, of course, because the phone has been disconnected. But, Mom, what's going on?" questioned Nia once again, as she held her mother's hand.

She could tell that her mom was withholding some information.

"Well, do you know that guy that was over here a while back?"

"Oh, that fat guy name Charles, the drunk."

"Don't call him a drunk, dear," said Racheal.

Well, he is a drunk, thought Nia and a crazy one too, if I may add.

"Is he your boyfriend?" queried Nia.

"Yeah, he was, but I have some good news, dear," smiled Racheal.

"What is it, Mom?" You broke up and will never see each other again, thought Nia wishfully.

"Charles and I just got married," replied Racheal. A big grin spread across her haggered face.

Hearing the news made Nia's heart sink. She knew the lousy bum was no good.

"Married! What do you mean, you two got married!" yelled Nia.

"We just got married at the court house, and we want you to stay with us. Charles and I talked about this the other night."

"What?" Nia said, unbelievingly. The idea of staying with her mother and Charles made Nia nauseous.

"I don't want you staying with the Thompsons anymore!" snapped Racheal.

"But I love it there. I like being over to Charlene's house," said Nia.

"Well, I can understand that, but we still want you to stay here with us. This is your home, and you shouldn't be over there all the time."

"But Mom-," Nia was close to crying.

"No, listen, dear! Listen to me! We're your parents now, Charles and I. And we want you to stay here with us. OK, and that's final! You're going to stay with us, and there's no questions asked, all right!" Racheal yelled angrily, pointing her finger in Nia's face.

Can't Mom see how she's shattering my world? Nia thought. Doesn't she care. I just can't stay here, it would be like living in hell, thought Nia.

"But Mom-!"

Racheal interrupted again, "Nia, I don't want to hear it!"

She folded her thin arms across her small breasts and said, "I want you to get your stuff from over there and bring it over here, because you're going to stay here with us from now on. And anyway, I miss you."

Racheal reached out her slender arms to Nia. Nia walked over and hugged her mom.

"I miss you too Mom," added Nia.

But, Mom you're a drug addict, you don't act like a mother, you always get high, and I never have a chance to talk to you, she thought. A million negative thoughts flooded Nia's mind.

Tears filled her pretty brown eyes. She wanted to tell her mom her thoughts, but she didn't dare.

"Anyway, Charles should be up here in a minute," said Racheal pleasantly. Evidently, she had no idea of how Nia felt about Charles.

"What happen to your eye?" queried Nia.

Her mom still didn't answer the question about her black eye.

Racheal gently touched Nia's shoulder and said, "Oh dear, don't worry about that."

He must have done it, Nia thought angrily.

Charles finally walked through the door, "So did you tell her the news?" he asked in a deep thunderous voice.

"Yeah, I told her," said Racheal giving him a long passionate hug.

"Nia, go give your new father a hug!" demanded Racheal.

"Aw, Mom!"

She didn't want to go anywhere near that nasty bum. Nia hated him with a passion.

"Do it! Now!" yelled Racheal with her hands on her hips.

Racheal walked out and went into the bathroom. Nia looked at Charles with a hateful glance.

"Give your daddy a hug," said Charles with a crooked smile on his face.

Nia looked at him and thought how disgusting he was. He looked so filthy and dirty, and she hated his nasty, drip, drop, jerry-curl. His hands were still very crusty looking. She didn't want to hug him, but she didn't want to hear her mom's mouth later on. One quick hug wouldn't hurt, she thought.

She was about to hug him when he reached quickly and pulled her closer to him. Next thing she knew, he was rubbing her back, and then his awful hands slid on down to her butt. Nia tried to push him away, but he was much stronger than she was. Charles kept on fondling her; he grabbed her breasts and kept on touching her butt.

Once she got one hand off her breasts, his other hand reached down and touched her behind. This whole ordeal was like a game to him.

"Stop it!" yelled Nia. She couldn't believe what was happening to her.

"Come here, girl," said Charles. She kept on trying to break away from his forceful grip.

"Please, stop it!" yelled Nia once again.

He started laughing at her. Nia began to cry because she felt so vulnerable.

She continuously tried to push him away, screaming, "Let me go!"

He whispered, "You might as well get use to this, Nia, and try to start enjoying it because-."

Charles finally let Nia go when he heard Racheal coming out of the bathroom. Nia quickly moved away from him in fear.

"You know your mom said that you are going to stay here, don't you?"

She noticed that he was looking at her in a very perverse manner. She knew that she was in danger when she was near this man, and the thought frightened her greatly.

Racheal was high and her mind was somewhere else. Whenever she gets stoned, she's not in tune with what's going on around her; she just gradually drifts off into her own little world, leaving me here alone and unprotected with this horrible man.

Nia answered, "Yeah, she did."

He winked at her and he moved a little closer. Nia moved away from him and stood closer to her mom.

So much was going through Nia's mind. He was her step father and he was fondling her. He grabbed my titties and my butt, she kept thinking in disbelief. All of this was pulling her world apart.

Nia looked away from him. The memory of him touching her and winking at her made her physically ill. She had to get out.

"Mom, I am going to the basketball game."

"OK, you be back with your things, now. From now on, you're going to be staying with us," slurred Racheal.

"All right," answered Nia weakly.

"I'll see you later, dear. Come give your mom a hug," slurred

Racheal. Nia hugged her and kissed her on the cheek.

Nia looked at her mom. "Are you sure you're all right?"

"Yeah, I'm fine."

Nia turned away and was about to walk out the door.

"Oh you are going to walk by me and not give me a hug?" Charles asked coarsley. She looked his way and then at her mother and walked swiftly out the door. She was not going to hug him, especially after what he had just done to her.

Nia slammed and locked the door. Closing her eyes, she whispered, "Damn, I can't fuckin believe this."

Desperately, she didn't want to stay with her mom, especially since Charles would be living there. If I'm ever left alone with this man, he will rape me, she thought. Nia knew she had to stay away from him. She had a lot of fear in her heart of what it would be like living with them.

Man, I have to do what my mom says because she is my mom, she thought. I've got to tell Charlene; I don't know if I can handle all this alone, thought Nia.

Finally she reached the subway station. Her long brisk walk was a blur, because so much stuff was clustering her mind. In the mist of troubled thoughts, she got on the train.

When she got to school. Nia spotted Charlene standing inside the front entrance. Casually, Nia approached Charlene.

"Hi, girl, how are you doing?" asked Charlene. A warm smile came across her cute face.

"Oh, I'm fine," sadly mumbled Nia.

Charlene could see that Nia was bothered and unhappy about something.

"Why are you looking so down and gloomy?" asked Charlene. She placed a caring hand upon Nia's shoulder.

"Girl, it's a long story," answered Nia.

"Really?"

"Yeah."

"Well we have about two hours before the game starts. Do you want to go to the subway shop, eat, and talk about this some more?"

"Sure."

"Let's go."

They reached the sub shop.

"Do you have any money?" asked Charlene.

"Oh, no, I don't have any money," answered Nia.

"Well, Mom gave me some extra money just in case you did not have any," added Charlene. Charlene reached inside her purse and pulled out a ten dollar bill and handed it to Nia.

"Your mom is so sweet."

"Yeah, she figured that you wouldn't have any spending money, so she told me to give you some."

"Aw, tell her thanks for me," said Nia.

Her statement took Charlene off guard, because she had thought Nia was coming home with her, so she said, "What do you mean, you can tell her tonight."

"I don't know if I'll be able to stay."

"Why?" asked Charlene, curiously.

"That's part of the long story I have to tell you."

"Oh, OK, we can talk about it over our sub sandwiches, then."

Charlene began to wonder what Nia had to tell her; it certainly seemed like bad news.

While in line placing their order, they talked about various things, mainly boys.

"So, have you seen Scott?"

"Oh, yeah, I saw him going down the hall at school with Miranda," answered Charlene.

"Oh, really?"

"Yeah he was still with that same girl we saw at the ice cream parlor a while back," answered Charlene.

"Well, maybe one day he will notice you, Charlene."

"Yeah, right, I don't think that he will ever know that I exist."

"What about you and that mystery guy, Nia?"

"Oh, yeah, that's one of the things that I wanted to talk to you about. Girl, I saw him today," smiled Nia.

"You did?"

"Yeah, I saw him when I was walking home. He was walking the other direction with his homies."

"Oh, really?"

"Yes, he looked so good, and I still don't even know his name."

"Why don't you go up to him and ask him his name?"

"Nah, I can't do that, I'm waiting for him to approach me first."

"Well, you may be waiting forever for him to approach you, girlfriend."

"That's true," admitted Nia.

"Isn't he going to play at the basketball game?" asked Charlene, as she recalled seeing him in a basketball jersey.

"I hope so," said Nia.

After receiving their food, they sat in a booth across from each other.

"Hmmm, this food smells good," said Charlene, sniffing the appetizing aroma.

"I'm hungry," added Nia.

Charlene was waiting for Nia to tell her about her news but Nia still didn't mention it, so Charlene finally asked her about what it was that Nia had to tell her.

"So what do you have to tell me?" queried Charlene, with a raised eyebrow.

"Girl, this is awful," answered Nia sadly. Her eyes became watery when she thought of going back home to her mom.

"Charlene, my mom wants me to move back in with her."

"What?" asked Charlene in disbelief.

"Isn't that awful?" asked Nia.

"Yes, it is. I can't believe this! Why does she want you to stay with her after she been dissing you? She's not much of a mama! Girl, I wouldn't go back if I was you," snapped Charlene, shaking her head with disapproval.

"Not only that, Charlene, she married that man."

"What man?"

"You know that man I told you about, the one she was getting high with a few months ago."

"Yeah," said Charlene, recalling having that conversation with Nia.

"Well, they got married," added Nia.

"No!" exclaimed Charlene. Her mouth flew open and eyes widened in shock.

"Yes, girl, they went to city hall and got married."

"Gosh, that's a real bummer."

"And not only that, Charlene, I can't trust this man."

"Really?"

Charlene took another sip of her soda to swallow down her food. She was dying to know why Nia couldn't trust the man that her mother married.

"Why can't you trust him?" she asked.

Nia looked down and started to cry. Charlene saw that Nia was crying, so she wiped her mouth with her napkin and moved to the other side of the booth to sit next to her friend. She put her arms around Nia to comfort her and gave her a napkin to wipe her tears.

"Why are you crying, Nia? This must be horrible!" queried Charlene.

Nia began to tremble.

"I'm scared, Charlene."

"Why are you scared, Nia?" asked Charlene with deep concern.

"Because I think he beats on my mother."

"Really? Did your mother tell you that?"

"No, but she had a black eye, and I believe he did it," answered Nia, taking another sip of her soda through her straw.

"How do you know if a drug dealer didn't do that?" asked Charlene.

Nia knew why Charlene asked that question. About three months before, a drug dealer beat up Racheal because she didn't have the money to pay him back for drugs she had bought on credit.

"I think that this time it's different, and I believe that he beats on her, I really do."

"Gosh," said Charlene amazed at all the awful news Nia was telling her. Charlene was wondering why on earth Nia's mother wanted her to move back with her after all this time she was trying to get rid of daughter for her own selfish reasons.

"And not only that, Charlene, when I went to hug Charles, he grabbed my butt." More tears rolled down her cheeks.

"He grabbed your butt, girl?" questioned Charlene in disbelief. She covered her mouth in shock.

"He was feeling on me."

"He did what? But this is molestation. Girl, you're only thirteen years old," whispered Charlene.

"I know," agreed Nia.

"Man, it would be different if he was your boyfriend, but this man is old. He is your step father. He shouldn't be doing this. And most of all, you should be able to trust him!" exclaimed Charlene.

Hearing all of this disturbed Charlene even more deeply.

"I know I shouldn't move back in with her, but I don't have muchof choice. My mom wants me to come back, and she has custody of me. Oh, I don't want to go back, Charlene!" cried Nia.

"I don't blame you. You got to find a way out of this, girl. You can't stay there."

"I know," Nia admitted sadly.

"Gosh, if that man was sick enough to feel on you, no telling what else he might do."

"I know, and that's why I'm so scared. If I move back home, I'm afraid he might rape me."

"If I was you, I would stay away. Who knows? She'll probably be stoned tonight, so she most likely won't know if you went home or not."

"Yep, she's probably high right about now; she always like to get high during the evenings," added Nia.

"Does she still look skinny, Nia?" asked Charlene after remembering how frail Nia's mom looked the last time she saw her.

"Yeah, she is as skinny as a rail, and she looks terrible."

"Girl, you can always come and stay with us anytime. You know that my mom always tells you that you have a home with us." Charlene gave Nia a loving hug.

"Nia it will be all right, everything will be fine, so perk up a little. If you are scared, you don't have to go stay with your mom. That's a sick old man, and he knew exactly what he was doing. Maybe we should tell my mother about this."

"No, no, please don't tell your mother," said Nia quickly. Nia was very embarrassed about the whole situation and didn't want anyone else to know about it.

"Why don't you want my mom to know about this?" asked Charlene. She thought that this was a serious matter and felt they should inform an adult.

"I just don't. I really don't think it's a good idea," answered Nia.

"Well, Nia, what are you going to do?"

"I don't know, I'm going to try my best to stay with you all. I like it over your at house. I feel like a part of the family," said Nia wiping the tears from her eyes with her napkin.

Charlene moved back to her side of the table. "Dang, girl, you have it bad."

"I know, but I'm going to figure something out. I'm not going to let this get me down," added Nia.

"I hope things work out for you," added Charlene, finishing up her sub-sandwich.

"Charlene, there's something else I have to tell you. I've been holding all of this in for a long time, and I do need to talk to someone about this."

"What is it?" asked Charlene as she leaned forward a little, to listen to what Nia had to tell her.

"This is not the first time that this has happened to me," said Nia as she looked down and wiped away the crumbs that had settled on her lap.

"What do you mean, Nia?"

"Well, I already told you that my mom always brought a lot of men over to screw for drug money."

"Yeah, I remember you telling me about it."

"Well, sometimes they would give me a nasty look like, if they had me alone, they were going to take advantage of me. Well, some of them did molest me, and one of them actually raped me before while my mom was gone. I have never told anyone this but you. I've kept this a secret."

"You mean to tell me you been molested and raped before?" asked Charlene. This explains a lot of things, thought Charlene. That's probably why Nia already knew so much about sex when she was just eleven years of age and was able to tell Mrs. Thompson everything, including graphic details. And this probably explains why Nia was so fully developed for her age.

"Yes, I have," answered Nia.

"Damn," uttered Charlene.

Charlene was so shocked about all this disturbing news that she couldn't say much of anything; she didn't know what to say to Nia.

"That's why I don't want to stay, because I just don't want this to happen to me again. And that's why I am scared of Charles, because of the terrible things that he may do to me," said Nia.

"I don't blame you, Nia. We need to find a way to get you out of this mess," said Charlene.

"That's the reason why I ran away from home when I was eleven and then again when I was twelve years old."

"That's deep girl, that is really deep," fretted Charlene.

Charlene felt sorry for Nia and really wanted to help her out, but she felt handicapped because Nia didn't want her to tell anyone else about her situation.

"Girl, let's perk up, let's talk about something else," mumbled

Charlene. The more she thought about the things going on in Nia's life, the more it bothered her.

"Yeah let's talk about something else," agreed Nia.

Nia knew that her eyes were red from crying so hard; she was glad she had a close friend to talk to because all of this was tearing her up inside.

"Yeah, now tell me about that guy you saw walking down the street."

"Yeah, girl, he looked so good. He's so fine and bow legged. I might try to approach him one day."

"Yeah, you should," added Charlene.

Charlene looked down at her plate and noticed that she had eaten all of her food.

"Well I'm finished with my sandwich. You didn't eat much of yours, you barely put a dent in it," said Charlene as she casually observed Nia's plate.

"I'm not hungry."

"Our earlier conversation must have made you lose your appetite."

"Yeah, it did," responded Nia.

"Don't worry, girl, things will get better for you."

"Yeah, I hope so. God is right by my side, and he will pull me through."

Charlene glanced at her watch and said, "Well, I guess we better go, it's already 6:00. We're supposed to be at the gym by 6:30."

Nia and Charlene slid out of their seats and left the submarine-shop. They walked back to the school together, each in complete harmony with the other. They came from two completely different worlds and, yet, they still managed to stay best friends.

This time, things seemed a little different. Charlene now held a deep dark secret that Nia had shared with her. Knowing this secret and sharing Nia's pain made Charlene feel like more than her best friend. From that day on, Nia and Charlene were more like sisters, both sharing each other's secrets and each other's pain in the struggle to gain inner strength.

Chapter #5

Meanwhile, Nia and Charlene reached the gym. They went downstairs to the girls' locker room and changed into their cheerleading uniforms. The game started at 7:00, and it was already 6:45. Coach Williams came into the locker room and blew her whistle to get the girls' attention.

"Now, girls, it is time for you to go upstairs to the gym, and I want you all to start warming up and practicing your cheers."

Nia and Charlene got their blue and gold pom-poms and went up to the gym. Moments later, the crowd began to appear. Finally, it was 7:00 P.M. and time for the game to start. The referee went to the middle of the gym floor with a microphone in his hand and began to announce all of the basketball players on both teams.

Tonight, Washington High School (Wild Cats) was playing Turner High School (Bulldogs). The referee called out the visiting team's name first. Turner's school colors were red and gold.

Many of the spectators in the stands booed the visiting team. After the referee finished calling out the visiting team's names, he called out Washington High School's basketball players.

"Richard Allen, Bryan Clark..."

As the referee called out the names, the spectators applauded

"Maybe you'll see your mystery guy," said Charlene as they were sitting on the bench and observing what was going on.

"Gosh I hope so," smiled Nia.

The gym smelled like popcorn. Outside, there was a concession stand that sold pickles, popcorn, soda, hot dogs, nachos, candy, and other tasty items. Nia loved the popcorn because it was buttery and slightly salty, just the way she like it. Smelling the popcorn in the air made her very hungry.

"I'm going to go to the concession stand to buy some popcorn and a soda," Nia told Charlene.

"Me too, girl I was thinking the same thing."

"I guess he doesn't play B-team basketball," said Nia as she watched closely to see if she could locate the guy she had a crush on.

"I guess not, cause I haven't seen him either," said Charlene.

Suddenly, Nia spotted him. On his jersey, it said number 21.

Just then, Charlene poked Nia with her elbow. "Girl there he is!"

Nia was staring hard at him and listening closely to what the referee was saying.

Nia watched as the mystery guy jogged to the middle of the gym and stood with his team mates; the players gave each other high fives and hit each other on the butt as they ran out to the middle of the gym.

The referee called out, "Clarence Walker."

So that's his name, thought Nia.

"Charlene, he's so cute!" exclaimed Nia.

"Calm down, girl," laughed Charlene.

"Man, he looks so good in his uniform," said Nia.

The basketball game finally began. The cheerleaders went to the sidelines and started cheering. Nia cheered very loud and did a backwards flip.

Throughout the game, the cheerleaders cheered with lots of enthusiasm, because their team was winning the game. They cheered, "Get fired up, get fired up, get-fired-up-Hey!"

The cheerleading squad later yelled, "Washington Wild Cats are going to win, but Turner Bulldogs are going to lose!"

The auditorium was filled with loud noise, as the spectators cheered for their teams. Turner High School was a prep school attended mostly by spoiled rich kids. Their cheerleading squad was very stiff and did mainly corny dorky-looking cheers that most people found boring.

Nia watched Clarence as he played. He dribbled the ball and passed it to one of his team mates. Clarence ran down the court with his hands in the air as he waited for someone to pass him the ball.

He caught the ball in his hand and then dribbled a little. Once he got near the basket, he leaped in the air and executed a perfect slam dunk. Nia watched him glide though the wind in slow motion.

She cheered even louder and jumped up and down every time she saw him score.

The speaker called out, "And Clarence Walker made a slam dunk, that's another point for Washington High School...so far, Clarence has scored 18 points for his team and now the score is 42 to 12!"

The crowd roared, "Go, Wildcats, Go!"

Every time Clarence made a slam dunk, the spectators yelled, "Go, Clarence, Go!"

Nia watched Clarence and loved what she saw. He was sweating and his rippling muscles glistened. His muscular hairy legs were gorgeous; every time he jumped or ran down the court, the muscles in his legs would tighten.

His hair was cut in a nice low hair cut filled with brushed waves. Nia wondered what it would be like just to run her fingers through his hair. She could image how soft it would be against her finger tips.

Since the cheerleading squad was so close to the basketball court, Nia had a chance to get a close look at him. Nia loved his intense brown eyes and lovely milk chocolate skin.

While Nia was cheering, Clarence walked right past her. Then he turned his head around to get a real good look at her. Man, that's the girl I saw about a month ago, thought Clay. She's real cute. He smiled at her, and she smiled back at him.

After he smiled, he winked at her. She looked around to see if he was winking at someone else. When she saw no one else looking at him, she pointed to herself; he nodded his head 'yes' to imply that he was winking at her. Nia began to blush; she was so glad that Clarence had actually noticed her.

The game was over, and Washington High School had beat Turner High, 60 to 20.

Meanwhile, Nia found Charlene and told her what had happened. "...And Charlene, he noticed me!"

"Girl, that is so great, I'm so glad for you. At least Clarence noticed you quicker than Scott would ever notice me. Gosh, girl, you must be head over heels over this guy. I see you learned his name," said Charlene.

"Yeah, I remembered it from when the speaker was calling out the names before the basketball game started," added Nia.

"Well, Nia, I'm going to walk out with Mary, I'll be waiting for you up front."

"OK!"

Nia turned around and went back inside the gym. She saw her

and pom-poms by the bleachers.

Then, she saw someone dribbling the ball, still practicing even after the game. It was Clarence, he still had on his basketball jersey under sweat pants and sweat jacket.

Nia thought about his muscular legs. He's so fine, she thought as she continued to watch. Watching him, she saw nothing but beauty.

Clarence turned around and spotted Nia standing near the bleachers. She was about to leave.

He called out, "Hey! Hey! Hey! Wait up!"

Nia turned around.

"Yeah, you," replied Clarence as he jogged towards Nia.

While approaching Nia, he took a good long look at her. Gosh, she's so beautiful! he thought. Her eyes were wide and soft and gentle, reminding him of a frightened fawn. Her hair, long and shiny, cascaded down past her shoulders, and her skin appeared to be almost flawless. All of a sudden, Clay felt shy as he was about to approach her.

He gazed into her eyes and said, "I've been noticing you."

Nia looked up at him and smiled. "What do you mean, you been noticing me?"

"Exactly what I said," grinned Clarence.

"Really?" asked Nia, disbelief showing in her tone.

"Yeah. What's your name?" Clarence looked down into her eyes.

Nia blushed and answered, "My name is Nia Chevez."

"Nia, that's a pretty name."

"Thank you," said Nia as she looked away for a brief moment. She was still amazed that she was actually talking to him.

"My name is Clarence, but most people call me Clay," Clay

continued to eye her up and down. Home girl is fine, he thought, she definitely has some big titties and pretty legs!

Nia looked up at him and admired how nice and tall and handsome he was. He has to be at least six feet, three inches tall, thought Nia.

"What grade are you in?" asked Nia.

"Oh, I'm in the ninth grade."

"Oh, really?"

"Yeah. What grade are you in?" asked Clay.

"I'm in the eighth grade."

"So you're a subie!" laughed Clay.

Nia noticed that he had the prettiest white teeth she had ever seen. What a dream! she thought.

"Maybe we can keep in contact with each other," said Clay, one eyebrow arched in hope that she wouldn't turn him down.

"Yeah, I would like that," smiled Nia.

Nia was embarrassed because she didn't have a phone; she was wondering whether or not to tell him about her phone situation. Well, what the heck she thought, if he really likes me, it won't matter whether or not I have a phone.

"Um, um, um...I don't have a phone," said Nia softly, looking down. Clay could tell that she was embarrassed.

"Don't worry about that; it's no problem. Here's my number," said Clay.

He wrote down his phone number on a piece of paper and handed it to Nia.

Nia was very impressed and surprised that it didn't bother him that she didn't have a phone, knowing this made her smile.

"Maybe we can go out sometimes? What are you doing after the game?" asked Clay.

"Well, Charlene and I were planning on going out for some pizza. Do you want to join us?"

"Sure, the fellas and I was thinking about going out for pizza too. Maybe we could go together as a group," suggested Clay.

"Yeah that's a good idea," agreed Nia.

"OK, well I'm going to see if my friend Marcus wants to go."

"All right, we'll meet you all out front."

"OK we'll be out there in a few minutes," said Clay, turning around to go back downstairs to the boys' locker room.

Nia knew that she was looking pretty. She had on eye liner and lip gloss that she felt made her look a little bit older. Her hair had lots of body and sheen; for the first time in a long time, she was having a good hair day. One side of her hair was pinned up in a comb, while the other side fell loosely on down past her shoulders.

After flirting with Clay, Nia went to the front of the gymnasium to meet Charlene. Nia spotted her sitting on a bench. She walked swiftly toward Charlene to fill her in on the latest news.

"Hi, Charlene," said Nia, trying to hold her excitement.

"Hey, girl, you just missed Mary. She left with Natasha."

"Oh, really?"

"Yeah."

"Guess what!" exclaimed Nia.

"What?"

"I saw Clay right before I came out here and he asked if Marcus and him could join us," said Nia.

"Great, that would be fun."

Five minutes passed on by. Clay and Marcus finally came out front. Laughing and joking, they headed to the Superb Pizza Restaurant on 21st Street. They had a wonderful time, and this was the beginning to a close friendship between Nia and Clarence.

Chapter 6

A week has passed by, and Nia had not heard from her mother. She was hoping that her mom had forgotten about the idea of her moving back home.

It was Sunday, February 16, 1984, and Nia and Charlene were getting dressed for church. Nia had her hair pulled up into a long pony tail and twisted it up into a thick ball. She had on a pretty light blue dress with small floral prints. Mrs. Thompson had given her the dress last Christmas.

Charlene was hot curling her hair.

"Ouch!"

"What happened?" asked Nia.

"I just burnt my ear with the curling iron," said Charlene.

"I hate it when I do that. I have burnt myself plenty of times doing my hair. Put some oil or cocoa butter on your ear," suggested Nia.

Charlene put some cocoa butter on her ear, "Wow, Nia it does feel much better!"

After getting dressed for church, Nia and Charlene went downstairs for breakfast.

Later, Mrs. Thompson finally came downstairs. Mrs. Thompson looked stunning. A healthy-sized woman with meat on her bones, her face was round with deep dimples on each cheek. She had on a sharp suit, it was beige colored with a nice hat to match.

"Gosh, Mrs. Thompson, you look real nice today," Nia complimented her.

"Why, thank you, dear!" said Mrs. Thompson searching through her purse for her keys.

"Charlene, do you have your Bible?" asked Mrs. Thompson.

"Yes, Mom, I have mines."

"How about you, Nia?"

"Yes, I have mines, too," answered Nia.

"Great, then we are ready to go. Come on, Joseph, let's go," said Mrs. Thompson as she located her keys and headed out the door. Joseph was so cute; he had on a navy blue suit with a red bow tie on the front of his white shirt. He was already snaggle-toothed, and every time he smiled, he showed it off. This year Joseph had started the first grade, and he thought he was real hot stuff especially since he knew how to read.

"Is Mr. Thompson going?" asked Nia.

"No, he has to work in the restaurant today," answered Mrs. Thompson.

"Oh, I see," responded Nia.

They got into Mrs. Thompson's gray Mercedes Benz. After buckling up, they were set on their short journey to Mount Zion Baptist Church. Mount Zion was a huge church that sat right on the edge of town. It was the biggest building on the entire block. The church's temple could be seen from miles away.

Finally, they reached the church and slid out the gray leather seats of the car. It was very cold and rainy.

Once inside, Nia could hear the gospel choir singing, so church service had already began. The usher at the door led them right on in and handed them a program.

They sat on the middle row of the pulpit and got settled down in their seats. Mrs. Thompson began to clap her hands and stomp her feet to the beat.

The choir had on their red and white robes, and the choir director swayed from side to side as he directed the choir. The drummer for the choir was a teenage boy named Steve who attended the same school as Nia and Charlene.

Mrs. Thompson was enjoying the music so much that she had to stand up and really get into the rhythm. Nia started clapping her hands. She loved listening to the up lifting sound of gospel music.

After the choir finished their selection, Pastor Peterson stood before the pulpit. He was a short stocky man with dark chocolate skin. He had a bald spot on the top of his head that shined every time the light hits it. Charlene and Nia used to joke about rather Pastor Peterson's glasses or head shined the most.

Once Pastor Peterson finished the altar prayer, he went right into his sermon. This Sunday, Mr. Peterson preached about faith and believing in God. Nia really focused on what he was saying; she found that hearing the word of God made her feel much better inside.

For some reason, Nia felt more at peace after praising the Lord. She had believed in God since the age of three. She remembered her grandmother, Maria Chevez, teaching her how to pray. Every night Grandma Chevez would have Nia get down on her knees right beside her and pray before she went to bed. Thinking about her grandmother, made Nia realize how much she really missed her. Grandma Chevez had died when Nia was nine years old.

After church service was over, they all went home and changed into somecomfortable clothes while Mrs. Thompson prepared collard greens, mashed potatoes, cornbread, and oven fried chicken.

Both the Thompsons were excellent cooks; people all over town loved to go to their soul food restaurant, Thompson's Sizzlin House of Food. It was definitely the big talk all across town.

Nia went upstairs to work on the book report she had to turn in on Wednesday; it was a report on Fredrick Douglas. The rich aroma of food from downstairs made her hungry. Charlene, already finished with her homework, she was downstairs watching t.v. with Joseph.

An hour passed by and Nia had finally completed her history report. She got up from the desk, feeling like she had accomplished something positive. A lot of times it was hard for Nia to just sit down and focus on doing her school work. Many times she just lost interest in what she was doing.

Nia raced down the stairs and headed straight to the kitchen.

"Hi, Mom," she said.

Hearing those words from Nia's mouth made Mrs. Thompson smile, because she thought of Nia as her other daughter.

"Hi, Nia, did you finish your report?" she asked.

"Yes, I did. Will you be able to read it later?" asked Nia.

"Sure, I'll do that after we finish eating dinner," responded Mrs. Thompson.

"Great! Is there something you need me to do?" asked Nia.

"Yes, you can make the salad and get the table set."

"OK, then," said Nia.

Nia was about to leave, but, Mrs. Thompson said, "No, better yet, go tell Charlene I want her to set the table while you do the salad."

"OK," said Nia as she walked out of the kitchen.

After washing her hands, she went to the den and told Charlene, "Your mom wants you to set the table while I fix the salad."

"Aw, man! I don't feel like it!" complained Charlene.

Nia left the den and went back to the kitchen. After she got the vegetables she needed, from the refrigerator door, she went to the sink to wash them clean.

While Nia was fixing the salad, the phone rang. Mrs. Thompson went to answer it.

"Hello."

On the other end of the phone was Racheal.

"Is my daughter there?" snapped Racheal.

"Yes, but she's busy now," answered Mrs. Thompson.

This made Racheal very angry. "Look, Nia is my daughter and I want to speak to her!"

"Look, Racheal! Haven't you hurt the girl enough?" asked Mrs. Thompson tiredly.

"Well, she is my daughter, and I want her to live with me."

"I don't think that's a good idea," said Mrs. Thompson.

"It doesn't matter what you think because, like it or not, she's going to be living with me and my new husband!" sneered Racheal.

"You just have to come into the picture and ruin everything don't you? Since she's been staying with us, her self esteem is so much higher and her grades have improved-."

"I don't have to listen to this bull shit!" Racheal interrupted rudely.

"Just tell her I want her to be here with her things by tonight!" angrily yelled Racheal.

Click. Racheal hung up the phone.

"Well I be damned," uttered Mrs. Thompson, realizing how ugly and rude Racheal was on the phone.

Nia heard Mrs. Thompson talking, and she knew it was her mother on the other line.

By Mrs. Thompson's facial expression, she knew that things were not good.

"Was that my mom?"

"Yes, dear, that was your mother," answered Mrs. Thompson sadly.

"What did she want?"

"She wants you to go back home with her tonight."

"What?" asked Nia in shock.

"Nia, she wants you to start packing up now and move back in with her by tonight," added Mrs. Thompson.

"But I don't want to go back. She doesn't care about me!" yelled Nia as she began to cry.

"I'm sorry Nia, but there's nothing I can do about it."

Nia fled up the stairs. Mrs. Thompson called after her, but Nia just kept going.

Charlene heard Nia getting upset and yelling so she went to the kitchen to see what was going on.

"What happened Mama? Why is Nia so upset?" asked Charlene.

"Nia's mom wants her to move back in with her, and she doesn't want to go back."

Charlene shook her head in disbelief.

"Why does that crackhead want her to move back in with her? All she wants is some extra money from the government and to sell Nia's clothes in the street so she can get more money for drugs."

"Now, Charlene, watch your mouth! Don't say that about her mother!" snapped Mrs. Thompson.

"Sorry, Mom, but I don't blame Nia for how she feels. I wouldn't want to go back, either."

After a while when Mrs. Thompson felt Nia had a chance to calm down, Mrs. Thompson knocked on the bedroom door.

"Come on in," answered Nia as she sat up on the bed and

wiped her teary eyes.

Mrs. Thompson walked in and sat on the other end of the bed.

"Nia, are you OK?" asked Mrs. Thompson placing her hand on Nia's shoulder to try and comfort her.

"Yes, I'll be fine. It's just that all of this came to a big shock, you know," Nia's words trailed off as more tears formed in her troubled brown eyes. Mrs. Thompson got up and walked over to the night stand to get a box of Kleenex.

After handing the box to Nia, she sat close beside her.

"About a week ago Mom told me that she wanted me to move back in with her and her new husband. I was hoping she would forget about the idea of me moving back in but she just had to call and ruin everything," mumbled Nia.

Nia was very comfortable with Mrs. Thompson; she felt that she could really talk to her about almost anything. Mrs. Thompson sat and listened as Nia poured her heart out to her. Listening to Nia made her teary eyed too.

Moments later, Mrs. Thompson spoke to Nia and tried to make her feel better.

"Nia, I know that all you are feeling right now is hurt, but you do have to go back to your mom because she does have custody of you."

When Mrs. Thompson told her that, Nia looked down at her lap and then looked away from her.

Mrs. Thompson waited a brief moment until Nia turned her head back around.

"I don't want to see you go, but I don't have any other choice. You know that you can always come and visit us and spend the night whenever you want," added Mrs. Thompson as she held Nia's hand.

Nia nodded her head and gently bit her lip as a gesture that she understood what Mrs. Thompson was saying.

    After their long discussion, they both went downstairs to join everyone at the dinner table. There was nothing but silence at the dinner table. Even little Joseph was quiet. Eating dinner that night was very strange; no one had anything to say. There was nothing but sadness in the air. Nia didn't eat much on her plate; she had lost her appetite.

    Once dinner was over, Nia went upstairs to pack. Charlene came into the bedroom to help her pack up the rest of her belongings.

    "Nia, why don't you want my mom to know about your dark secret? If she knew that you have already been raped by one of your mother's male friends, she wouldn't let you go back to her," said Charlene while folding one of Nia's sweaters to go inside her suitcase.

    "I know, but I just don't want her to know. Charlene, you must keep this a secret, nobody must know about this. Please don't tell anyone," pleaded Nia.

    Charlene looked at Nia and could tell that she was determined about this whole thing; she couldn't understand why Nia didn't want anyone knowing about such a serious matter.

    "But Nia, I really do think that this is a serious matter and someone should know about what's going on," added Charlene with concern.

    "Charlene, I just don't want anyone to know about this. All of this is very embarrassing, and I don't want it to be known. Let's just forget about it , OK?" insisted Nia, forcing the rest of her clothing inside the suitcase.

    Charlene knew that Nia was getting angry and frustrated, so she didn't push the issue any further. They went downstairs with the suitcases and then outside to the car. Mrs. Thompson was already waiting in the car; she cranked it up and backed out of the drive way. The drive to Nia's house was very quiet. The only sound that could be heard was the purring of the engine.

Finally they reached Hooper Homes. Mrs. Thompson parked about two blocks from the complex because she didn't want her Mercedes Benz to get broken into; she made sure all the doors were locked before she left.

All four of them, including little Joseph, walked in the cold dreary weather. It was two blocks to the dark rusty gates that led to Hooper Homes. Inside, some old drunken men with beer bellies were hanging out, gulping down their liquor, and getting geeked up; one of the men was Charles.

On the basketball court, some guys were playing basketball; while in the dark filthy alleys of the complex, some illegal dealings were going down. In the background, Nia could hear the sirens of police cars and ambulances driving through the war zones of the night.

Nia looked at Mrs. Thompson and could tell she was scared. Eventually, they reached the building where Nia lived. Nia opened the door and they followed her inside. As they went up the stairs, the steps made a loud squeaky noise. Mrs. Thompson turned up her nose when she saw all of the foul language written all over the walls and roaches crawling everywhere; she covered her nose when she smelled the awful strong smell of urine; some nasty person hadn't even bothered to go to the bathroom.

At last, they reached the top of the stairs; slowly, they walked to Nia's apartment. Nia knocked on the door and in a moment, Racheal answered the door. Racheal stood in the doorway with a cigarette in one hand and her other hand placed on her narrow hip.

"Oh Nia, how's my baby? I've miss you so much!" exclaimed Racheal as she reached out and hugged her daughter. Mrs. Thompson noticed that Racheal was completely ignoring their presence; she didn't speak to them or even bother to acknowledge them.

"Hi, Racheal, we brought Nia over for you," remarked Mrs. Thompson, holding Joseph's hand in hers.

"Oh hi," Racheal replied shortly.

Four years ago Rachel asked Thelma to keep Nia because she knew that she was neglecting her child. A social worker threaten to take Nia away from her if she didn't straighten up. Depressed and strung out on drugs Racheal begged Thelma, her dearest friend, to let Nia to stay with her until she got her act together.

That little old rich bitch, thought Racheal, she thinks that she's everything since I asked her to take care of Nia for a while. She thinks that Nia is her own child, thought Racheal. Thinking about all of this made Racheal's heart burn with fury. She looked down at Mrs. Thompson's son. He's a cute little chocolate colored kid, she thought.

"Is that your son?" asked Racheal with a stern expression on her face.

Before Mrs. Thompson could answer, Racheal released the smoke that she had inhaled from her cigarette and some of the smoke went into Mrs. Thompson's face. This made Mrs. Thompson angry because she knew that Racheal had done it on purpose.

Racheal sneered when she saw Mrs. Thompson's facial expression.

"Yes, this is my son, and we're going to leave because I see we're not welcomed here," responded Mrs. Thompson.

"Ain't that's the truth," rudely remarked Racheal, rolling her eyes.

Nia was very upset about the way her mom was acting; Racheal didn't even bother to invite them inside.

"Bye, Nia, I'll see you later," said Mrs. Thompson, and both Charlene and Joseph waved good bye.

"Bye, Mrs. Thompson. I love you," Nia said brokenly.

A moment later, Nia rushed after Mrs. Thompson and gave her a hug; she held on so tight that Mrs. Thompson had to tell her that she had to let go.

Nia began to weep.

"Come on, Nia, you need to come back inside. You're home with your real mama now," snapped Racheal.

Nia wiped her eyes and waved goodbye and went back inside.

Chapter #7

The same night Nia moved back home with her mother, something very strange and peculiar happened. Nia got herself ready for bed that night. She pulled her long thick wavy jet black hair into a bushy ponytail. After taking a shower, she put on her favorite purple and white pajamas with a unicorn on the front. She lay down in her small twin size bed and drifted to sleep.

After hanging out with his buddies for most of the evening, Charles went back home. He unlocked the door and walked through the kitchen. While in the kitchen, he placed his coat and hat on the coat rack. Swiftly he walked to the bathroom; he was in a serious tight.

While washing his hands, he took a good look at himself in the mirror; he didn't like what he saw. His eyes were red like cherries and his drip drop jerry curl sagged down in his face. He looked down at his large beer belly, and he just stood there and rubbed it for a moment.

Not too long ago Charles had been an attractive man, but drugs and alcohol had drained his good looks and destroyed his world. His mind drifted to Nia. She's so young and beautiful, he thought. He opened the door and looked down the hall to the door to Nia's bedroom. Slowly, Charles walked toward Nia's bedroom. He reached the door and placed his hand on the knob and turned it. He walked on

in and saw Nia curled up in her bed. Awh, isn't that precious, thought
Charles. The moonlight fell right inside Nia's room, so he could see
her very clearly.

Charles stood there watching her for a while. Nia stirred and
turned her head. She looked up and saw a figure standing in her
doorway. She wiped cold from the corner of her eyes and then looked
again, she realized it was Charles standing there. Seeing him standing
there gave Nia the creeps. She sat up quickly and wrapped her blanket
closer around herself. Charles closed the door behind him and then
approached her.

"What do you want?" asked Nia.

"Shhh," whispered Charles with his index finger to his lips.

"Stay away from me!" demanded Nia.

"Shh," whispered Charles once again.

He sat on Nia's bed and placed his hand over her mouth. With
his other hand, he hastily unbuttoned her purple fleece pajama top.
Nia tried to push him away from her but he was too strong. She tried
to scream but his hand was held firmly over her mouth.

Finally her breasts were exposed, and he started rubbing them
with his hands. Charles was rubbing her breasts so hard that they
began to ache. He bent his head down and started sucking on them.
Nia began to cry. While roughly sucking her breasts, his hands moved
down to her butt and then between her legs. Charles was hurting her.

He pulled down her pajamas bottom and panties. He continu-
ously fingered her and made her very sore. After fondling her for
twenty straight minutes, he let her go. Nia moved to the corner of her
room and curled up in fear.

Charles grinned and said, " See you later, sweet thang."

With that, he winked at her. Nia stayed in the same corner for
the rest of the night and cried herself to sleep.

A week passed. Almost every night, Charles came into Nia's bedroom and took advantage of her. He threatened her and told her not to tell anyone.

One late afternoon, Nia decided to tell her mom what was going on. Coming home from school, Nia went into the living room, where her mom was. Before saying a word, Nia checked the entire house to make sure Charles was not home. He was not there, so Nia decided to have a talk with her mother.

As usual, Racheal was puffing on a cigarette and watching sometalk show on T.V. Racheal was staring off into space; Nia could tell that she had just awakened from being high.

Nia gently tapped her on the shoulder, "Mom, there's something I have to tell you."

Racheal stretched and then looked at her daughter and smiled.

"Yeah what do you want, child?" asked Racheal.

"I want to tell you something about Charles."

"What about him?"

"Mom, he's been, he has been feeling on me," said Nia.

"You said what!" exclaimed Racheal.

"He's been touching me in places that are wrong," added Nia.

Hearing this made Racheal angry. She didn't believe Nia. She reached out and slapped Nia across her face.

"How dare you make up such a damn lie! He's your stepfather. You're just jealous and don't want to see me happy!" yelled Racheal.

Nia rubbed her cheek because her face stung from the slap. She started to cry, because she knew in her heart that she was telling the truth.

"But Mom, I'm telling the truth," pleaded Nia.

"Go to your room and I don't want to see your face again, you no good heffa!" sneered Racheal in fury.

Nia left the room and went to her bedroom. She was hurt that her mom didn't believe her. Knowing this drilled a hole right through the middle of her heart.

The next Saturday night, Racheal told Charles that she was going to the store to get a few groceries. There was no more booze in the house, so he asked her to pick up some liquor from the package store.

"Racheal, will you get me some mo liquor while you're out?" asked Charles.

"Sure I'll get some. Where's the dough?" asked Racheal, reaching out her hand.

"I'll go get it," answered Charles.

Charles went to the dresser in their bedroom and got his wallet. He took out a ten dollar bill and gave it to Racheal. After receiving the money, Racheal walked out the door.

About two hours went by, and Racheal returned. Charles went to the kitchen when he heard her at the door.

"Hi, did you get it?" asked Charles.

Racheal started giggling and laughing. Right then and there, Charles knew that she was high.

"Where's my money!" yelled Charles.

"It's all gone!" giggled Racheal.

After hearing her answer, he kicked her in her stomach with so much force that Racheal was knocked violently to the other side of the room.

"Who in the hell gave you the right to use my fuckin' money on some damn crack?" roared Charles.

From next door, Nia could hear all the commotion. She was at her friend, Laporsha's, house.

"Is that your folks fighting again?" asked Laporsha, who could hear them arguing, too.

"Yeah, that's them. I'll be right back," responded Nia.

Nia got up from the couch and went home. Through the door, she could hear Charles yelling and cursing her mother.

After fumbling for her keys in her pocket, she unlocked the door. Nia was very shocked at what she saw; Charles was holding Racheal by the hair and continuously punching her in the stomach like a punching bag. Blood came out her nose and mouth. She had been beaten so severely that she was unconscious.

Nia ran rapidly towards Charles. She leaped on his back and started punching him as hard as she could. None of her punches inflicted pain. Instead of hurting Charles, she made him more angry. He grabbed Nia and threw her full force across the room. Nia hit the wall so hard that she was knocked out.

When Nia finally woke up, she saw a strange man with a little flashlight gazing into her eyes. It was a doctor checking her out to make sure she was OK. Nia tried to get up, but her head started to spin.

"Don't try to get up so fast. You're suffering from a mild concussion."

"Where's my mother?" asked Nia.

"She's down the hall getting stitched up," answered the doctor.

"I'm Dr. Kawaski. Here's an ice pack to put on the back of your head to relieve some of the pain and swelling."

"Where am I?" asked Nia as she rubbed her neck.

"You're at Mathis General Hospital," answered Dr. Kawaski, "and you're all set. Now you can go into the waiting room and wait on your mother," he added with a nice warm smile.

Nia slowly got up and walked to the waiting room. Her head

was still hurting really badly, so she placed the ice pack back on her head. Once she found the waiting room, she sat down in one of the chairs. A few minutes later, a police officer approached Nia and asked her a few questions. Nia look at his name tag, and it read Officer Hicks.

"Was your stepfather the one who beat up your mother?" he asked.

Officer Hicks was a medium built white man with brown hair and clear blue eyes. He appeared to be in his late twenties or early thirties. He looked very serious and was all about business.

Nia answered, "Yes, he was the one."

"We have arrested your stepfather," said Officer Hicks.

After asking a few more questions for his police report, he left.

Later that night, Nia and Racheal were released from the hospital and took a cab home. Nia was happy that Charles was in jail because he would not be messing with her that night. The next morning, Charles called Racheal and begged her to get him out of jail. He promised that he would not beat her or Nia again, and she believed him. Racheal fell for Charles' tricks once again, so she went to the police station and dropped all the charges. Charles was eventually released from jail.

Three weeks passed by, and Charles was still coming into Nia's bedroom at night. She was tired of him hurting and touching her on the wrong parts of her body. Nia wanted desperately for all of this to stop.

One day after school, Nia went to a hardware store and purchased a lock for her bedroom. She set the lock so she could lock the door from inside, so no one could come in her room without a key. She needed a lock not only to keep Charles from molesting her, but also to keep Racheal and Charles out of the money that she was saving. They often stole Nia's hard earned money, from working at the Thompson's restaurant, for drugs.

Night rolled around. After Nia got dressed for bed, she locked her bedroom and dozed off to sleep. Suddenly, she was awakened to the noise of Charles at her door. He tried to open the door, but it was locked. This made him very angry, and he knocked on the door so hard he made it shake.

Nia jumped when he hit the door with so much force. She was terribly frightened.

"Nia, I know you're in there, so open up the fuckin' door and let your daddy in," thundered Charles.

Nia did not answer; she was too scared.

Charles continued to pound on the door and tried to open it, but was unsuccessful. Tears rolled down Nia's cheeks; she feared that Charles would get the door open and do her a lot of harm.

Just when she thought he would get in, Charles gave up.

"That's all right, don't open the fuckin' door!" he yelled furiously while kicking the door.

"Just remember that your ass is mines in the morning. You're gonna get a good old fashion ass whipping just like I gave you and your mother the other night!" roared Charles.

Nia shivered. She wished badly that she was still staying at Charlene's house; she had felt so safe over there.

Nia decided that she was going to sneak into the bathroom in the morning and make sure Charles was nowhere in sight when she left for school. And in the afternoon, she had no intention of going back home. She would spend the night over at the Thompson's house in an effort to avoid being beaten up by Charles. After analyzing what had just happened and planning what she was going to do, Nia went to the sleep.

Sunlight crept into Nia's room. From outside, she could hear the sound of cars and people out on the streets. She yawned and stretched and rolled over to look at the clock to see what time it was; it was 7:15, and it was definitely time to get ready for school.

Nia got up and walked towards the door. Before going out of the door, she placed her ear against it to see if she could hear Charles around. When she didn't hear or see anything after peaking out the door, she opened it wider and tip-toed out quickly and quietly to the bathroom. Before she could reach the bathroom, Charles intercepted her with a dirty smirk on his face!

Nia looked up at Charles in fear. Her eyes were wide and her mouth sprung open in shock. The first thing Nia could think of was running. She turned around and started running. Charles quickly caught her and yankedly her by her pony tail. Then he started dragging her ruthlessly down the hall by her hair. Nia screamed in pain. Both of her hands went up to her head in an effort to try to keep him from pulling her hair out.

Once he dragged her to the kitchen, he started slapping her violently across her face. Eventually, his slaps turned into punches. He punched her several times across the jaw and in the stomach. He grabbed her arm and yanked it hard; Nia heard her bones pop. Then he kicked her twice in the stomach and once in the back.

"Now I told you, bitch, that in the morning I was going to give you a good old fashion ass whipping for locking that door last night. Everytime you lock the door, the more you are going to get beat down!" yelled Charles pointing his finger at her.

Charles rumbled through the drawer and pulled out a knife. He slashed her legs with it and stormed out of the house.

Nia didn't move for a while because she was in so much pain.

She couldn't move her left arm. All she could do was lay there and cry.

Slowly she lifted herself up and limped to the bathroom. She looked at herself in the mirror: her face looked horrible; he beaten her until she was literally black and blue.

Nia was very upset at the reflection she saw in the mirror. She was so upset that she banged her fist against the mirror with rage. Her eyes was swollen, her lips were bloody and busted open, and her nose was bleeding. She could barely move because her stomach and back were aching so badly. Whenever she tried to take in a deep breathe, she felt excruciating pain in her abdomen and lower back.

With a damp face cloth, Nia cleaned herself up. After cleaning the blood off her face and arm, she went back to the mirror to see if she looked any better; she still looked awful, and she knew that she couldn't possibly go to school looking like this.

For three straight days, Nia had not been in school and Charlene was very worried. She couldn't call Nia because their phone was disconnected. Charlene knew that she had to go over to Nia's house to see if she was OK.

Charlene really missed hanging out with Nia. Lately, Charlene noticed that Nia had been acting strangely; she had been very quiet and more to herself. Nia's style of clothing had also changed. Instead of wearing her usual cute feminine outfits, she wore baggy clothing. Dressed in her loose attire, she seemed ashamed of her body.

Charlene was very concerned about Nia's change in behavior. She knew that something bad was going on at her house and she was worried about what it might be. She decided that she was going over to Nia's house to see what was going on.

That evening, Charlene went home and spoke to her mom

about Nia.

"Mom, I'm very concerned about Nia."

"Why are you worried about Nia?" asked Mrs. Thompson sitting on her bed to tie her tennis shoes. Mrs. Thompson was getting ready for her Thursday night aerobic class.

"It's seems to me that she's been acting very strange lately. She's been very quiet and to herself. And you know that's totally unlike Nia."

"Well dear, maybe it's taking her a little more time to adjust to moving back in with her mother," Mrs. Thompson was standing in front of the mirror combing her hair. She knew that Charlene was probably right about Nia's living situation being something to worry about.

No telling what's going on with that poor child, thought Mrs. Thompson; not too long ago, Nia had told Mrs. Thompson about how in the past her mom had brought over a lot of men at all hours of the night and about how some of those men had come on to her when she was only eleven years old.

Mrs. Thompson really felt bad for Nia, but she didn't want to get involved again. She remembered how badly Racheal treated her when she brought Nia back to her house. Mrs. Thompson knew that Racheal was not in the least thankful that she had taken care of Nia when she was not able to do so herself. She was unable to be a good mother to Nia, because she was always out in the streets. She simply loved crack more than her own daughter, thought Mrs. Thompson.

"Mom, I'm so worried about Nia because she's missed almost a week of school. And I can't get in contact with her because their phone is still disconnected," blurted out Charlene with a worried expression on her face.

Mrs. Thompson looked at Charlene and could tell that she was

Mrs. Thompson looked at Charlene and could tell that she was really concerned. Charlene was talking so fast that Mrs. Thompson had to stop for a second to absorb all she said. Mrs. Thompson finally agreed to go with Charlene to check on Nia. "OK Charlene, I will not go to aerobics class tonight. We will see about Nia," responded Mrs. Thompson.

"Thank you Mom!" Charlene gave a sigh of relief and gave her mom a hug.

Charlene's worst fear was that Nia was being sexually abused. More than anything, she wanted to tell her mom Nia's dark secret, but she had promised that she wouldn't tell a soul about the abuse that Nia had gone through and was going through right now.

After having their brief conversation, Mrs. Thompson and Charlene got in the car and headed towards Nia's house. Little Joseph didn't go with them, because Mr. Thompson had taken him to a Boys Scouts meeting.

Finally, they reached Nia's side to town. Mrs. Thompson once again parked her car a few blocks from the projects, and they walked to Nia's complex in a worried silence.

They climbed the dark dreary staircase and ultimately reached Nia's apartment. Mrs. Thompson knocked on the door, and when there was no reply, she knocked again. A moment later, they heard footsteps on the other side of the door.

Nia was in her bedroom when she heard someone at the door. At first, she didn't get up, but the second time she heard the knocking, she slowly got up from her bed. Still aching and sore she dragged herself to the door. Gosh, I wonder who that could be, thought Nia.

Once Nia got to the door, she looked through the peep hole to see who was there. She discovered that it was Charlene and her mother. She was so thrilled to see them.

Nia reached for the handle to unlock the door, but she was a little hesitant to do so because of the way she looked. Her face still looked terrible from the beating Charles had given her; both her jaws and eyes were swollen, one of her eyelids would not open, and her lips were still badly cut and bruised.

Slowly she opened the door and stood behind it when she let them in. Nia closed the door behind them.

"Hi, Nia, how are you doing?" asked Mrs. Thompson. Nia's back was still turned to them; she was very ashamed about the way she looked.

"Oh, I'm doing fine," slurred Nia.

Mrs. Thompson noticed there was something wrong in the way Nia sounded.

"Well girl, aren't you going to come around here and give us a hug?" asked Charlene.

"Yeah," answered Nia.

She turned around as if she didn't want to be seen, but both of them finally saw Nia's face.

"Oh my God, Nia! What has happen to your precious face!" exclaimed Mrs. Thompson in shock as she approached Nia.

Mrs. Thompson gently cupped Nia's face with both her hands, and tears filled both their eyes.

"Who did this to you?" asked Mrs. Thompson.

"My stepfather," answered Nia.

"Mom, Nia needs to go to the hospital!" Charlene screamed.

"Yes she does," agreed Mrs. Thompson through gritted teeth.

Seeing Nia looking like this made Mrs. Thompson very angry; she couldn't understand how any adult could have done such awful things to a child. Mrs. Thompson knew that Nia could not stay in that place any longer. She decided to take Nia home with her once again.

"Come on Nia, you're going with us," said Mrs. Thompson.

Nia winced in pain as she tried to walk to her room to get her clothes. Reaching to help her, Mrs. Thompson saw that Nia was cut badly on the leg.

"Charlene, go get Nia's clothes please, because she's unable to walk to her room," said Mrs. Thompson. Mrs. Thompson helped Nia walk to a chair so that she could sit down. A few minutes later, Charlene came back in the living room with Nia's things packed and ready to go.

Mrs. Thompson knew that Nia had it rough, but she didn't know things were this bad.

"OK, Charlene, you carry Nia's things while I help her walk," Mrs. Thompson said grimly.

Slam! The door closed shut behind them.

Chapter #8

Finally, Mrs. Thompson, Nia, and Charlene reached Mathis General Hospital. After signing Nia in, they waited for a doctor to examine her. Two hours passed before a doctor saw her.

The doctor was an attractive, thirty-something, brown skinned woman.

"Sorry for the long wait, but we've had a lot of people rushed in here this morning."

She looked at Nia's chart and then at Nia.

"So you're Nia? How did this happened?" Holding Nia's chin, the doctor scrutinized Nia's busted lips and swollen eyes.

"I got beat up," slurred Nia.

"Nia, I'm Dr. Young, and I'm going to take good care of you, OK?" smiled the doctor.

"OK," said Nia.

"A nurse will be with you in a few minutes, and I'll be back shortly."

Dr. Young thought it was posible that this was another case of child abuse; she decided to do a little research to see if Nia had been there before for similar injuries. Based on her experience in dealing with child abuse, she had a feeling that Nia had been physically abused by an adult, perhaps by one of her relatives.

A nurse came and directed them to a room. It was a very cold room, so cold that it made Nia shiver all over and raised chill bumps on her arms. Slowly Nia walked around and sat on the hospital bed. She noticed that almost everything in the room was white.

After Dr. Young finished examining another patient, she went to her office to retrieve some information from the computer on Nia. Once she retrieved her file, she printed it.

Later, Dr. Young went to the file room to obtain Nia's confidential medical records. Quickly glancing through the papers, she discovered that Nia had been at this same hospital on numerous occasions for similar type injuries.

She found that Nia had been seen by two different doctors. It seemed as though Dr. Young's theory about Nia was correct. Dr. Young knew for a fact that Nia has been to this hospital before for injuries, such as having stitches, bruises, and mild concussions, since the age of nine. It seemed very suspicious that this child was going through some type of abuse at home. Dr. Young took off her glasses and rubbed her temples with deep concern.

After taking fifteen minutes to find out this piece of information about this child, she headed down to her room.

When Dr. Young reached Nia's room, the nurse had already cleaned Nia up and examined her deep cuts and bruises. Sabrina, the nurse who took care of Nia, approached Dr. Young in the hallway before she reached Nia's room.

"It looks like she's going to have to get some more stitches," said Sabrina.

"You mean to tell me you've seen this patient here before?" asked the doctor.

"Yes, I believe about a month ago both her and her mother were here to get treated for injuries. I think she had a minor concussion," answered Sabrina.

"Do you know who did that to her and her mother?"

"I'm not quite sure but I do know one thing, her stepfather was the one who got arrested," replied Sabrina.

"Really? Do you recall who the doctor was that examined her?"

"I believe it was Dr. Kawaski," recalled Sabrina as she looked down at her medical charts.

"OK, thanks, Sabrina. I appreciate you helping me out with this information," said the doctor as she walked briskly away.

Dr. Young entered Nia's room.

"Hi, Nia, how are you doing?"

First the doctor examined her stiff arm.

"Nia, try to move your left arm."

Nia couldn't move it.

The doctor moved the arm slightly and Nia yelled "Ouch!"

"Oh, dear, I'm afraid your arm may be broken." said Dr. Young.

"I'll need an x-ray of her arm," Dr. Young told the nurse assisting her.

The doctor sat down on a stool to take a closer look at Nia's facial bruises and deep cuts. She also examined the bruises that covered the girl's entire back.

The doctor gently pressed down on her back and asked, "Does that hurt?"

"Yes," flinched Nia as she felt a sudden surge of pain.

After examining her closely, Dr. Young took Mrs. Thompson aside and asked, "Are you her mother?"

"No, I'm her godmother. I watch after her whenever her mom is unable to or just don't feel like being bothered with her," answered

Mrs. Thompson.

"Do you know where her mother is?" asked Dr. Young.

"No, she's out in the streets somewhere."

"Do you know if there's any way to contact her?"

"No, they don't have a phone. I don't mean to be nosey, but Nia is very important to me. Why do you need to contact her mother? Is she going to be OK?" Mrs. Thompson had a worried look on her face.

"She's going to be fine, Mrs. Thompson. You have nothing to worry about. But her arm is broken and she's going to need some stitches and some pain killers Mrs. Thompson, do you know how long she's been in this condition?"

"Well, she told me that she was beaten up about a week ago, and she has not been to a doctor because nobody has been home to take her until we came today. We discovered her in this condition."

"Do you know who did this to her?" asked Dr. Young, taking off her glasses.

"Yes, she told us that her stepfather did this to her."

Hearing this information deeply disturbed the doctor; remembering that Sabrina had also mentioned the stepfather earlier.

"All right, then. She has to get some stitches and have a cast put on her arm. We can't wait to reach her mother so we're going to go right on ahead," added Dr. Young.

"OK," said Mrs. Thompson.

Dr. Young had to first pop Nia's bone back into place and put a cast on her arm; it was a painful experience for Nia but she took it very well.

Dr. Young knew that the deep cuts on Nia's forehead and leg had to hurt; even after five days, they had not yet began to heal. She quickly started working on the wounds.

Mrs. Thompson and Charlene went to the waiting room while Dr. Young and the nurse stitched Nia up. After working on Nia for about an hour and thirty minutes, Dr. Young came into the waiting room to speak to Mrs. Thompson.

"Hello, Mrs. Thompson, we've finished with Nia and right now she is resting," smiled Dr. Young.

"That's great. Did you have to put in a lot of stitches?" asked Mrs. Thompson. "All together we did eighty stitches. It appears that her stepfather may have used a sharp object to cut her this badly," responded the doctor.

"Can we go see her?" asked Charlene eagerly.

"Sure," answered Dr. Young.

Later, the police came and asked Mrs. Thompson, Charlene, and Nia questions. Nia refused to press charges on her stepfather because she was afraid he would harm her mother. He told her that if she was to ever press charges against him, he would kill both her and her mother. Charlene and Mrs. Thompson couldn't understand why she wouldn't press charges; they tried to talk Nia into doing it, but this only upset Nia even more, so they left her alone.

The next day, Nia was released from the hospital, and Mr. and Mrs. Thompson took Nia to their house. Mr. Thompson came that morning when he heard what had happened to Nia. After taking Nia home, Mr. Thompson had to go back to the restaurant, but Mrs. Thompson stayed to make sure Nia was OK.

Nia didn't go back to school for another week. Charlene brought Nia's homework and class assignment home for her to do, so she wouldn't fall too far behind in school.

Throughout the week, many people came by to visit Nia. It really brightened her day when Coach Williams came to see how she was doing. The word was out at school that Nia was hurt and had to go to the hospital. Even some of the girls from the cheerleading squad came by to visit her.

Nia was really surprised when Clay came by to see her.

Mrs. Thompson went to Charlene's room and said, "There's someone here to see you, Nia."

Nia sat up slowly; she got out of bed to put on her housecoat and went downstairs to see who was there to see her.

When she got around the corner, she saw Clay sitting on the couch looking as handsome as ever.

"Hi," softly said Nia.

"Hello," grinned Clay. He got up to help Nia sit down on the couch.

"Gosh, I'm so surprised to see you," smiled Nia.

"Yeah, I couldn't miss out on seeing my beautiful buddy. I really miss you at school. I was wondering what happened to you."

"How did you know I was hurt?"

"Charlene told me." Clay looked at Nia. She had a huge bandage on her forehead and a cast on her left arm.

"Does it hurt?"

"Yes, a little bit," Nia glanced down at her arm and then looked at Clay.

"Word around school has it that you've been in a car wreck or got into a fight. There's so many rumors out about what happened to you that I don't know what to believe," Clay leaned back comfortably on the couch.

"Does it really matter how it happened?" asked Nia.

"No, but we're good friends. Why are you being so secretive about this whole thing?" Clay leaned over to take a good look at Nia.

Nia noticed how pretty Clay's eyes were and wanted desperately to talk about something else.

"So, Clay, how's your girlfriend?" asked Nia, trying to change the subject.

"Who? You mean Sonya?" laughed Clay.

"Yeah, Sonya," smiled Nia. Nia was happy that she had been able to change the subject.

"Well, we broke up."

"Really? What happen?" Nia was shocked to hear that, because Clay and Sonya had been dating each other for over a year.

"Both of us were getting tired of each other, so we decided to go our own separate ways," answered Clay.

Finding out that Clay had broken up with his girlfriend made Nia very happy. She knew this was selfish, but she had always had a crush on Clay and wanted to be with him, but was too afraid to tell him.

Later that evening, Clay left. Talking to him had really made her feel better. She was happy that they had such a strong friendship. A lot of times, they walked home together from school because they both lived in Hooper Homes. During their walks, they conversed about many things. Often, when walking, they made eye contact and smiled at oneanother in a way that revealed their strong feelings for one another.

Three months later, Nia had her cast taken off, and she was still staying with the Thompsons. Racheal had started calling on the telephone and raising hell about Nia living with them. After exchanging a few harsh words towards one another, the Thompsons decided to let Nia go back home right after her birthday, on February 6th.

Mrs. Thompson knew that Nia's birthday was coming up so she wanted to do something special for her. On Friday, the day after Nia's fourteenth birthday, the whole Thompson family got together and threw Nia a surprise birthday party. Right after Nia and Charlene came back from the mall that evening, Nia got the surprise of her life.

As Nia and Charlene walked towards the Thompson's apartment building, they noticed that the lights were off in the living room from the street and no cars were parked outside.

"Gosh, that's strange, nobody's home," observed Nia.

"Yeah, I guess they had to go somewhere," said Charlene as they walked up the steps.

Charlene reached down inside her purse and pulled out the keys to unlock the door. The door made a squeaky noise as she opened it.

"It's dark in here, let me turn on the light," said Nia.

Once Nia turned on the light, she heard voices of other people in the room.

"Surprise!" yelled everyone who was hiding behind the corner.

Nia turned around and saw all of her friends, all the people she loved and cared about.

Nia was more than surprised, she was flabbergasted.

"Happy birthday Nia!" smiled Mrs. Thompson, giving her a big warm hug.

Nia was so happy that tears came to her eyes. She hadn't had a birthday party since Grandma Maria gave her one when she was nine years old.

Gradually, Nia looked around at the small crowd to see who was there. She saw Mary and Laprosha. To her right, she spotted Clay and Marcus standing near the table with the food on it; as usual, the two of them were ready to dig into the food.

"We got you, didn't we?" laughed Charlene when she saw the surprised look on Nia's face.

"Yeah, you all really surprised me with this one," smiled Nia.

"Nia, come on over here and blow out the candles on your cake," called Mrs. Thompson as she gestured for Nia to come over.

Mrs. Thompson knew exactly what kind of cake Nia liked: strawberry short cakes. On top of the cake, it read, "Happy Birthday Nia." Nia looked down and counted the fourteen candles.

"Make sure you make yourself a wish," sang out Mrs. Thompson.

Nia made her wish; she closed her eyes and wished for a good future. After making her special wish, Nia opened her eyes and blew out all the candles. Everyone cheered and clapped. Then, they dug in and ate plenty of food. On the table, there were Buffalo wings specially prepared by Mr. Thompson with his secret sauce. There was also pizza, finger sandwiches, potato chips, dips, vegetables, cake, and punch. The aroma of the rich foods made everyone hungry.

In the background, music was playing on the entertainment center. All of Nia's friends had brought cassette tapes over. Most of them loved listening to Micheal Jackson's Thriller album, some Run D.M.C, and some jams from Atlantic Starr.

After eating, everyone went into the den, to dance. Clay, Marcus, Brandon, and Raymone competed with each other, showing off their break dancing moves; everyone stood around and watched them dance. After that, everyone started dancing themselves and had a real good time.

About thirty minutes later, someone turned on some slow dance music. Clay looked around to find Nia; she was no where in sight. Clay checked the kitchen and there she was, helping Mrs. Thompson wash some of the dishes.

"Can I dance with the birthday girl?" asked Clay, looking at Nia.

"Well-," Nia stumbled.

"Girl, go dance and have some fun! This is your party. I can handle cleaning up," laughed Mrs. Thompson with her hands on her hips.

Without saying a word, Clay took Nia by the hand and lead her to the den. It was very dim in there. Once they got to the middle of the floor, they started slow dragging. Nia looked around and spotted Charlene dancing with a guy name Robert. Clay placed his arms around Nia's waist and she put her arms around his neck. The song was "Sexual Healing" by Marvin Gaye.

Although, Clay really liked Nia and wanted her for more than just a friend, he didn't have the balls to tell her. He loved how she felt in his arms; she was so soft. He liked feeling her breasts brushing gently against his solid chest.

He whispered in her ear, "You smell so good." Hearing this made Nia blush. He lifted his hand from her waist and gently ran his fingers though her long soft hair. He had always wanted to do that; he thought she had gorgeous hair. She looked up and smiled at him, and he smiled back. She's so beautiful, he thought.

Nia wore tight Jordache jeans, a purple sweater, and white Reebocs. Clay's hands moved down to her butt and gently grabbed it. Nia felt uncomfortable, so she moved his hands back to her waist. He knew right then and there that she didn't want him feeling on her, so he stopped.

Clay wanted badly to kiss her, so he decided to be bold. He tilted his head down and gently kissed her on the cheeks. He noticed that she was very receptive to the kiss, so he decided to go for the gusto and kissed her on the lips. The kiss was very passionate, sweet, and gentle. Nia started to feel strange vibes that she had never felt before, and she kissed him back. Their intimate moment was broken when a rap song began to blare through the room.

Clay looked at Nia real hard and lead her outside. They went to the roof of the building and sat down on the steps to talk. The sky was very clear, and the moon and stars shined ever so brightly in the sky. It was about 30 degrees, so Nia put on her coat to keep warm.

"Nia, there's something I've been wanting to tell you," said Clay, turning to look at her. He reached over and took Nia's hand, looking deeply into her eyes.

"What do you have to tell me?" Nia smiled softly, fingering the lapels of his Starters jacket.

"Well, it's not exactly what I have to tell you, but what I want to ask you. Will you be my girlfriend?" Clay's voice was nervous and shy.

"I thought you'd never asked," smiled Nia. "Of course, I will!"

"Really?" asked Clay unbelieving.

"Yes," said Nia while nodding her head yes.

"Great!" yelled Clay as he stood up.

Clay reached down with his hands and helped her to stand up.

"You just don't know how much this means to me. Nia, since the first time I laid eyes on you, I always wanted you to be mines," he held her hands tightly in his. Clay pulled Nia closer to him and hugged her. He kissed her gently on the lips which gradually lead to a delightful french kiss. This was Nia's first real kiss by anyone she really cared about.

At 12:30, Nia and Clay went back inside. Almost everyone was getting ready to leave, except for some of Nia's girlfriends who were staying for the slumber party. The girls stayed up all night, watching horror movies, stuffing themselves with popcorn and soda, and talking about various things, mainly boys. The next morning everyone was tired and bleary eyed.

After the girls left, Charlene and Nia cleaned up the house. On Sunday, Nia left once again to live with her mother.

Opening the door, she laid down her suitcases and yelled, "Mom I'm home!"

There was no reply. She picked up her suitcase and carried it to her room.

While putting up her clothes, she sensed that she was being watched; she turned around. In the doorway, Charles was standing there watching her. He was giving her the same nasty stare as before. He began to eye her up and down and started to approach her.

Quickly she moved away from him and asked, "What do you want?"

Charles didn't answer her question. Instead he gave her an insinuating smile.

When she saw that awful smile, she started to cry because she knew what he was going to do.

Quickly she started running for the door, but Charles was too quick. He grabbed her, picked her up, and then threw her on the bed.

She yelled, "Mom! Mom!"

Laughing, Charles sneered, "What can your mom do? Don't you know I'll beat her ass too? Besides your mom's not here!"

Nia was so scared, her whole body shivered with fear.

"We're here all alone and I can do whatever I want to you," Charles grinned cruelly, his face inches from hers.

Nia turned her head away because his breath was foul with alcohol.

Charles grabbed her face and forced her to kiss him. Nia continued to cry and tried to get him off of her. He started slapping and hitting Nia violently, and then he raped her.

Chapter#9

In 1985, Nia ran away from home; she was fed up with the abuse.

Once Nia made up her mind to run away, she started saving up her money and hid it from her mom and stepfather. She found a job at a local grocery store and quit working at the Thompsons's restaurant; she knew that if Mrs. Thompson found out she had run away, they would only let her stay with them for a while and then send her back home to Racheal and Charles.

Nia had begun to feel like she was a burden to the Thompsons. She had overheard Mr. Thompson telling Mrs. Thompson that he thought Nia should stay with her mother. Nia knocked on their door one night to tell them good night, and there was no answer. She cracked open the door and peeked in, and she heard them fussing about her.

"Nia is not our daughter and not our responsibility! We should stay out of their family affairs, and let them work it out themselves!" argued Mr. Thompson.

"But honey, I love Nia like she's our own-."

"But she's not our own, don't you see that?" interrupted Mr. Thompson.

Nia quietly closed the door. Once she realized how Mr.

Thompson felt about her, she knew that she could never again go to them for help. She decided to take matters into her own hands.

For months, Nia made her plans and saved her money to run away. She found a cheap room in an old run down tenement building. She had to share a bathroom with four other people.

Even though her room was certainly not a luxurious place, Nia managed to call it home. When she first moved there, the room was filthy; the place literally had a ton of roaches. Nia cleaned the place from top to bottom.

Meanwhile, Nia and Clay were still dating each other. At first, he was very confused and had mixed feelings about Nia. He knew that Nia had a rough life, and he wished that she would open up to him and trust him more.

Clay was a wonderful friend to Nia; whenever she needed him for anything, he was there for her. She felt that his love had given her the strength to change her life. There were many times when she felt that, if it were not for Clay, she could not go on.

Eventually, Clay understood why Nia ran away from home and chose to live by herself. He really couldn't blame her, because if he were in her same situation, he would have done the same thing.

He knew about Nia's awful situation at home and he was right by her side through the whole thing. When they first started going together, he didn't know how things were at her home. Sometimes he saw bruises on her arms and would ask her about it. Finally, Nia told him the truth about everything.

At first, Clay was enraged; he didn't like the idea of anyone hurting her. He hugged Nia real tight in his arms and told her that no one was going to ever hurt her again, not as long as he was living.

Clay knew that her stepfather was a lousy drunk and her mom was a crackhead. As far as he was concerned, they both didn't give a damn about Nia. At first, he wondered why Nia didn't want him to meet her parents, but now he knew why: Nia was very ashamed of what she had to live with and didn't want other people to know about her family situation.

Often, Clay visited Nia's room; he considered it his second home. Clay was very attractive to Nia. She loved looking into his beautiful brown eyes which glittered like jewels. Clay was tall in statue. At sixteen, he was already six feet, five inches tall. Not only was Clay tall, dark, and handsome, he was also fine; he was very athletic and strong. Nia loved watching him exercise and flex his rippling muscles.

After dating each other for almost a year, Clay started pressuring Nia about sex. She was fifteen years old at the time.

One day, Clay and Nia was in her room chilling out after eating some Burger King. They moved from the table and sat down on her bed to watch T.V.

They enjoyed T.V. for about an hour, watching "The Facts of Life" and "Different Strokes". Clay stared at Nia intensely. She had on a peach colored blouse and blue jean mini skirt to match. Nia had taken off her penny loafers and unbuttoned the first two buttons on her blouse. Clay wished she would unbutton some more, so the he could get a better view of her breasts.

Nia leaned back on her elbows and crossed her legs. Clay watched her every move. Gosh, she's so fine, he thought, looking down at her shapely legs. Nia's eyes were still glued to the television.

Clay stared at the side of her face and noticed the dimples on her cheeks; her dimples showed every time she smiled or laughed. Nia looked up every once in a while and saw that he was still staring at her. When she caught him looking at her, she would smile at him.

Bump this, I'm going to make my move, he thought.

Clay leaned over and kissed Nia on her cheeks and then passionately on the lips.

Nia playfully pushed Clay away from her and said, "Clay, come on now, I'm trying to watch T.V." Then she looked at him and smiled. Clay thought she was joking and trying to play hard to get.

Clay leaned over and kissed Nia some more, but this time he placed his tongue in her mouth and gently intertwined it with hers. His hand moved down to her breasts; he gently squeezed and caressed them. Nia was scared. She was not ready for his advances, and she tried to push him away from her. Even though he felt her resist, he continued; his hand moved down to her butt.

He stopped kissing her on the lips and began to gently kiss her on the neck. Nia enjoyed his touch but she was still afraid.

"Clay, please stop, I'm not ready yet."

"Come on, baby, I'll be gentle," said Clay's voice was very deep and sexy.

Slowly his hand moved up her skirt; he gently caressed her soft thighs.

Suddenly, Nia had a flashback of her stepfather raping her. She started crying while Clay was on top of her.

"Get off me!" yelled Nia as she started hitting Clay.

Clay grabbed her hands to keep her from hitting him.

"Nia, what's wrong with you?"

Nia was so overwhelmed with fear that all she could do was cry.

"I'm sorry, Clay, but I can't."

Clay got up from the bed and turned off the T.V. set. He was very hurt and upset that Nia would diss him like that.

For a long time, he had been nothing but nice and patient with Nia, he was getting sick and tired of her crying everytime he came on to her. He tried to be understanding with Nia, but sometimes he found it hard to understand her. The only reason why he was still with her was because he loved her.

"Damn it, Nia, all I have been to you is fuckin patient with you! I'm getting fed up with this bull shit!" Clay paced back and forth across the floor as he yelled angrily.

"I'm sorry, Clay," Nia apologized tearfully.

"Nia, it's not like I haven't been there for you. I've been nothing but good to you. All I'm asking from you is to love me back and to give me some pussy every once in a while."

Clay sat down next to Nia. He knew why Nia was so afraid; he knew about her step father sexually and physically abusing her. He started to feel guilty because he felt that he may have been too hard on her. He looked at her and noticed that she was shivering and was still teary eyed. Clay hated to see Nia looking so sad.

He reached over and placed his arms around her for security. He gently rubbed her back and Nia laid her head on his shoulder. Clay reached in his pocket and pulled out a tissue.

"Here wipe your eyes," said Clay. Nia took the tissue to wipe her tears.

For a few minutes, Clay comforted Nia and continued to hold her gently in his strong arms. Nia felt so safe and warm in his arms that she almost fell asleep.

In a soothing voice, Clay said "Nia, making love is something special that is shared between two people, and that special something is what you and I share. I love you a lot, Nia. You're my baby, and I want this to be a beautiful experience that you will cherish for the rest of your life."

What Clay told her really touched her heart and she felt that what he said was truly sincere. Nia decided that she would go ahead.

and open up to him. She wanted to put her unfortunate rape experience behind her and move on with her life.

Clay leaned over and kissed Nia passionately on the lips, slowly unbuttoning her blouse. His kisses turned into sweet wet kissed along her neck.

Later, he took off her bra. For a few minutes, he stared at her lovely butterscotch breasts. His strong hands began to caress her breasts. He fondled her breasts and started to suck on her erect nipples. Slowly his hands moved underneath her skirt and caressed her soft firm inner thighs. His touch felt wonderful to her and made her wet between her legs.

Once Nia was completely nude, he stood up and took off his shirt. His abdomen rippled with muscles, and his biceps were tight. Clay had broad shoulders. He took off his blue jeans and underwear. After he finished undressing, he laid down beside her.

Clay got on top of Nia and started to kiss her entire body. He began to put himself inside her, but Nia stopped him.

"Wait, Clay, I don't want to get pregnant!"

Clay gently placed her finger over her soft lips and said, "Shh, Baby I'm not going to get you pregnant. I'll put on a condom." He reached in his blue jeans pocket and pulled out a Trojan.

After putting on the condom, they began to make love. Nia was mesmerized by love and passion. She didn't know that a man's touch could be so gentle and loving. Slowly he entered her and started to get busy.

The beautiful act of making love came to a standstill. After the experience of making love with Clay, she realized that what he was saying was right. Clay was a great lover, and he knew how to kiss, lick, and caress her in all the right places. The experience was very beautiful, and it was indeed something that Nia would remember and cherish the rest of her life.

Chapter #10

During Clay's senior year, he received a basketball scholarship to Duke University. Clay's mom was so proud of him because he was going to be the first one in his family to go to college.

Clay really loved Nia and hoped to marry her someday and have children. Sometimes Nia and Clay would spend time looking up at the stars and dreaming about their future; they both were determined to leave the projects. Clay felt that going to college was going to be his ticket out of the ghetto.

Unfortunately, Clay had a serious downfall: he still liked to hang and associate with the wrong crowd.

On the evening of April 16, 1986, Nia had a bad feeling about Clay hanging out with his friends, so she begged him not to go out. She wanted him to stay with her that night in her room. Clay told her that he would be back later.

"Me and the fellas are going to hang out for a while and chill over a case of beer," he said.

Clay turned around from the mirror after checking himself out. He looked up and saw the expression on Nia's face. From the look she gave him, he could tell she didn't want him to go.

"Come on, Baby, you have nothing to worry about. You look so worried. I'll be right back." And with that, he smiled and gave her a big hug. He gently ran his fingers through her soft hair and looked into her beautiful eyes.

Nia looked away from him for a moment. She had a lot on her mind. She had been to the clinic that day and found out that she was pregnant. In a way, Nia, was hesitant to tell Clay the news because she didn't know how he would react to it.

"What's the matter Baby?" asked Clay noticing the worried expression on Nia's face.

"Clay, it's just that I have something to tell you."

"Aw, Baby, can't this wait?" asked Clay hastily.

"Well, I guess it could wait," said Nia softly as she folded her arms in front of her.

Nia looked away from him, and Clay could tell she was a little sad about him not listening to her, but he had plans to hang out with his friends.

"OK, then I'll be back in a few hours. Now, Baby, you need to take that sad look off your face. It's not like I'm leaving you for good."

He placed his arms around Nia's waist and said, "Now give your Big Daddy a smile." Nia finally smiled and laughed at the silly expression he had on his face.

"Good Baby, now that's what I like to see, that pretty smile of yours."

Clay looked down at Nia and leaned over to place a soft loving kiss on her lips. His hands slowly lowered down to her butt and with that he whispered in her ear, "You know what we're going to do when I get back. We're going to get busy tonight."

Nia smiled and tip toed to place a sweet kiss on his cheek. Clay's deep, dark, dreamy looking eyes stared right into hers.

"I love you, Nia."

"And I love you too."

"I'll see you later."

"Bye."

The door closed shut right behind him.

About an hour after Clay left, there was a drive by shooting at his hang out spot. Clay was on of the victims who got shot.

It took the ambulance and the police a long time to get to the crime scene. Nia heard the gun shots and ran outside to see what had happened. She saw Clay lying on the ground.

She screamed, "Clay! Oh my God, no!"

She kneeled down by his side and told him that everything was going to be all right. She was thankful that he was still alive. Clay's sweatshirt was soaked in blood.

He looked up at Nia and tried to talk, "I'm cold."

Nia took off her coat and wrapped it around him. She looked down at him and saw that he was continuing to bleed very heavily.

Nia yelled with impatience, "Damn it! Why is it taking the fuckin ambulance so long to get here?"

With tears in her eyes, she told him, "Baby you will be all right. I love you so very much and I don't want you to die."

Clay looked up at her and smiled and began to cough heavily.

"I love you, too, Nia. I know that sometimes I don't show it and say it, but I really do."

Nia gently wiped tears from Clay's eyes. Seeing him in this condition hurt her deeply; she wanted so badly to take the pain away.

"Nia, I want you to have my silver jeep," whispered Clay.

"Clay, please don't talk that way. Baby, you're going to make it. You have to because I found out that I am pregnant with your child when I went to the clinic today, and that's what I wanted to tell you earlier."

Clay smiled at Nia, "If it's a boy will you name him Clay Jr.?"

"Why, of course, I will," Nia sobbed.

"Nia, the baby is going to be a boy," whispered Clay.

"Shh, Shh, you need to be quiet and rest. I know it hurts when you talk, because the pain is written all over your face," said Nia softly as she placed her finger over his lips to silence him.

Nia continued to hold Clay in her arms very tightly and tried to keep his trembling cold body warm.

Clay began to wince in pain. Finally, Nia heard sirens. The police and ambulance had taken an hour to get to the crime scene. Nia felt nothing but rage because it took the police and the ambulance too long; it just seemed like it take them extra longer to reach low income black communities, thought Nia.

Nia kissed Clay on the lips and told him that everything was going to be fine. She held his hands and his hands started to tremble. Nia knew that he had lost a lot of blood, and that was making him very weak. Three of Clay's friends had also gotten shot; Greg had died instantly after getting shot in the head.

Clay was finally put into the ambulance and rushed to the hospital.

Chapter #11

After reaching the hospital, Clay was rushed to emergency surgery. His mom came immediately when she heard her son had been shot.

About an hour after Clay was taken into surgery, the doctor came back and told his mom her son was dead.

She began to scream, "Oh my God! No, Lord, please, not my son!"

Mrs. Walker, Clay's mom, was a tall, largely built woman with plump jaws. After hearing the news of her son's death, she grew deathly pale. Nia and the doctor helped her sit down. Nia placed a cool cloth on her forehead.

Mrs. Walker sat in the chair in a daze; she couldn't believe that her baby was gone. Nia continued to wipe her forehead with the cool damp cloth.

"Thank you Dear," whispered Mrs. Walker.

She was crying nonstop. Nia hugged her and started crying too.

"Oh, Nia, what am I going to do?" asked Mrs. Walker in grief.

A week later, Clay was buried on May 3, 1986. The entire community attended Clay's funeral. At school there was a moment of silence for Clay.

Almost every night Nia cried over Clay. Not a day went by that she didn't think of him. Nia missed Clay so much that she didn't know how she could make it without him. She was also afraid; she didn't have a clue as to how she was going to support their unborn child.

After Clay's death, Racheal was put in the hospital; she overdosed on crack. Due to the high level of toxic drugs in her system, Nia's mom went into a coma. The doctors told her that they didn't know if Racheal was going to make it. Charles visited Racheal only one time in the hospital.

Even though Racheal was not always there for Nia as a mother, Nia was still there for her as a daughter. Almost every day, Nia came by the hospital to visit and to pray over her mother.

While Nia was visiting her mother in the hospital, she was almost five months pregnant, and she was going through a lot of stress, heartache, and pain. It seemed to her that life was nothing but a mass of confusion.

Unfortunately, Nia was not getting the proper prenatal care that she needed, because she simply couldn't afford the cost of doctor bills. Nia was not taking good care of herself, and often she found herself very tired and weak from not getting enough rest. She was always busy, either working at the grocery store, going to school, or trying to see about her mother. Due to depression, she was not eating enough food to feed her baby. Instead of gaining weight, she began to lose.

Nia really wanted to have the baby; she felt that it was the most precious gift that Clay could have given her. Mrs. Thompson wanted Nia to get an abortion. She felt that at sixteen Nia was too young to try to handle all of the responsibilities of being a single parent. Nia didn't listen to Mrs. Thompson's advice; she wanted to have Clay's baby.

Nia felt that this child was a piece of Clay, and she had promised him that she was going to have his baby right before he died.

Two weeks later, on August 15, 1986, Nia went into labor and had the baby prematurely at five months. Nia had a little boy and she named him Clarence Walker Jr., she named him after his father. Clay Jr. was very tiny and weak.

The baby was born so early that his brain, heart, and lungs were not fully developed. Clay Jr. was put in an incubator and plugged up to a machine that pumped his tiny heart for him. Nia was constantly at his side. She felt so bad because she couldn't even hold him in her arms; the only thing she could do was hold his tiny hands. Clay Jr. had tubes all over his fragile body and needles stuck inside his tiny veins.

Mrs. Thompson came to the hospital to give Nia some support. Nia was so glad that Mrs. Thompson was there for her in her turmoil; she didn't know what she would have done without her.

Baby Clay fought for his life, but on August 25, 1986, the struggle ended, and his heart stopped beating. The doctors couldn't revive the tiny infant. Her baby's death ripped Nia's heart apart.

Mrs. Thompson saw Nia's pain and tried to soothe her. She inspired Nia to go to church more often, and Nia evenually gained her strength from the light of the Lord. Nia had Clay Jr. buried right next to his father's grave. After the burial of her son, Nia had enough power to move on with her life.

Chapter #12

On November 20, 1986, Judge Harris let the Thompsons adopt Nia into their family. Mr. Thompson had a change of heart and wanted Nia as his daughter. When he found out that her stepfather was abusing both her and her mother, he wanted to help Nia get out of that terrible environment.

When Racheal went into a coma and was later considered brain dead, Charles tried to get custody of Nia. The Thompsons hired a lawyer and fought him in court and won.

They were able to prove that Charles was an unfit father due to his alcoholism, use of illegal drugs, violent temper, and physical abuse. The doctors who had examined Nia when she was beaten up by Charles were in court; the doctors testified to the the physical evidence that proved that Nia had been abused by her stepfather. Even Dr. Young was there to help Nia out.

Coach Williams took the stand because she had seen bruises over Nia's body on two different occasions when she was dressing out for P.E.; Coach had also tried to help Nia by calling a social worker from the school to go talk to her family.

Nia was very happy that she was officially a part of the Thompson family. Now, she didn't have to ever worry again about going back home to her stepfather and living in fear. Nia finally felt safe, knowing that she was truly home with a good family who, without a doubt, loved her.

Mrs. Thompson arranged for Nia to go to a counselor for therapy. She wanted to make sure the scars from Nia's troubled background were beginning to heal, both mentally and emotionally. For so long, Nia had held all her deep feelings of pain inside, and Mrs. Thompson knew this could not be healthy.

Through group therapy, Nia got much better. The group was made up of other teenaged girls who had been sexually and physically abused.

Through the group sessions, Nia had an opportunity to open up and share her deepest thoughts with the other members. Hearing other people's stories and situations encouraged Nia to share hers, too. Nia felt better knowing that she was not alone.

One day, out of the blue, Nia asked Mrs. Thompson a question while driving back home from the grocery store.

"Mrs. Thompson, there's something I've been wanting to ask you."

"What's that, Dear?" asked Mrs. Thompson while driving.

"Well, since you have adopted me, can I call you Mom and Mr. Thompson, Dad?" asked Nia.

"Why, of course, you may. We want you to call us Mom and Dad," replied Mrs. Thompson, smiling.

Mrs. Thompson was so happy that Nia wanted to call her mom, it made her burst with joy. Once they pulled into the driveway, Mrs. Thompson reached over and hugged Nia. From that day on, Nia no longer called her Mrs. Thompson, but, instead, she called her Mom.

Nia still kept the silver Jeep Cherokee Clay had left her. He had bought it right before he died; the jeep had tinted windows, a music system, and an alarm system.

After Nia graduated from high school in June, 1987, she decided to go to technical school, since she didn't do too well academically while attending high school. Nia really didn't care for school much, but she knew that going to school would be her ticket to prosperity, as Clay used to put it.

Charlene did very well in high school. She also graduated in 1987, and she graduated in the top ten percent of the class; Charlene's GPA was 3.8 and she received a full four year scholarship to Howard University. Nia was so happy for her, although she knew she was going to desperately miss her old friend.

Mr. Thompson paid for Nia's education. He really wanted her to go to a university but he couldn't talk her out of going to a technical school. Nia can be so stubborn when she wants to be, thought Mr. Thompson. He knew that Nia didn't like school at all, so he was at least thankful that she had decided to do something positive with her life.

While Nia was attending technical school, the decision was made to unplug Racheal from life support system; Nia's mom died on September 12, 1987. Nia didn't really mourn over her mom's death; she felt that she had lost her mom when she got hooked on drugs. Having a mom who was addicted to crack and who acted as if she didn't exist had badly hurt Nia. Nia felt like she had lost her mom a long time ago.

Right after Nia finished technical school, she found a job as a dental hygienist. Once Nia got her job, she moved out at age twenty. Her mom didn't want her to move, but Nia felt it was definitely time for her to go out and to experience the real world. For a year, Nia worked in the dental office while living in New York. Even though Nia was out on her own, she still didn't go out much. Ever since

Clay's death, Nia had not dated anyone seriously.

Nia was getting tired of New York's cold snowy winter weather, and she didn't like living the fast city life where people were always on the go. Nia wanted to go somewhere new. All her life she had lived in New York and had never been any place else.

She longed to see beautiful golden beaches and palm trees. She wanted to go somewhere where the weather was warm and pretty year around. Nia wanted to go to a place that wasn't as congested with people. She decided to leave and go to San Diego, California.

Chapter #13

While on the plane to San Diego, she thought about her past. Nia felt that she had gone through a lot for a twenty-one year old, and most people said she was very mature for her age. Whenever she thought about the rough times in the projects of Brooklyn, New York, she knew that she has come a long way.

Nia's concentration was broken by a flight attendant asking her, "Do you need anything?"

"No thank you," smiled Nia.

When the flight attendant left, she returned to her deep thoughts.

The year was 1990, and Nia knew that she was starting a new beginning.

She lay back in her seat and stared out the window. Outside, she could see the soft fluffy clouds floating gracefully against the beautiful clear blue sky.

She felt that God was constantly reaching out to her and telling her to move on with her life. Nia looked down at the gold cross pendant on the necklace her mom had given her right before she left New York.

She smiled and said to herself, "California, here I come."

Chapter #14

Nia got off the plane with the other passengers. She got her luggage and went outside to catch a taxi. The taxi driver helped put her luggage into the trunk of his cab.

Once she got in, the driver asked her, "Where to?"

"I would like to go to the Holiday Inn on Spring street,"

"OK."

The cab driver squinted through his rear view mirror to get a good look at her. He was captivated by her beauty: She was light skinned, had lovely full lips, a beautiful smile, and a great body. He had noticed her cleavage when she leaned over to help him put her luggage inside the car. Her hair was very long, and silky, cascading down her shoulders.

The driver asked, "Now, what is a beautiful young thang like you doing traveling alone?"

"I'm not traveling. I'm planning to move here."

"Oh, I see."

It was a fifteen minute drive from the airport to the hotel. The driver again helped Nia with her luggage.

"Thank you. How much do I owe you?" asked Nia.

"For you, fine thang, only five dollars." He grinned through crooked teeth.

She gave him the money and walked away. He stood there for a moment to admire her from a distance. Once she disappeared, he got back inside the cab.

Nia approached the front desk and asked the clerk about her hotel reservations. He gave her the keys to her room, and she carried all her luggage up to her room.

Once she reached her room, Nia walked right in and turn on the light. She saw a single bed and, to her right, an the empty closet with wire hangers.

Nia put down her luggage and, because the room was very dim, she adjusted the blinds to let in some light.

She went over to the bed and sat down. She ran her hand over the comforter and looked down and observed its lovely floral patterns. She picked up the remote control and flipped through the TV channels until she saw "The Young and The Restless".

Nia lay down on the soft bed and relaxed. Soon she was asleep.

She awakened much later. She looked down at her watch and was amazed to see it was already 5:00. Nia got up from the bed and stretched. For some reason, her muscles were sore and aching; maybe it's from the long flight, she thought.

Nia slid the glass doors open and stepped out onto the balcony. She stood there for a moment and enjoyed the beautiful scenery. The weather was wonderful in San Diego, about 80 degrees outside. A gentle breeze gently blew though Nia's hair, sweeping it from her face.

She stood there, in tranquillity enjoying the beautiful weather of southern California. She watched the palm trees gracefully sway from side to side, as the soft breeze continued to blow. It was very sunny and very bright outside. The beautiful view made Nia's day seem brighter.

Up the street Nia noticed the Golden Arches. The rich aroma of food made her realize that she was hungry. Nia's stomach started growling. She grabbed her purse and headed toward McDonald's.

Outside the hotel, Nia stood for a moment and took in a deep breath. There were gorgeous palm trees everywhere plus she could even hear the sound of the ocean, the sound of rushing waves and the cry of sea gulls in the near distance.

Everywhere she looked, everyone was in summer gear: people of all ages in shorts, T-shirts, swim suits, and bikinis. At McDonald's Nia ordered a fish-fillet sandwich, small fries, and a medium orange drink.

Once she got her food, she took her French fries out of the bag and started munching on them. McDonald's has the best fries, she thought to herself. Ever since she was a little girl, she could remember the times when she used to practically beg her mother to take her to McDonalds. Most of the time, her mom gave in because she always fell for Nia's puppy dog look.

Back at the hotel, Nia sat down at the wooden table, turned on the television with the remote control, and finished eating the rest of her food.

Nia wanted to get out of her clothes and take a shower. She got up from the bed and got undressed; she stepped into the tub and bent over to adjust the water temperature for the shower. She turned the knob for the shower and the water emerged from the faucet. The warm water felt wonderful against her skin.

While enjoying the shower, Nia had a chance to relax and think about things. She knew that she had to call her mom and tell her that she had arrived safely. Her mom didn't want her to leave New York, but she was still supportive of Nia's decision.

After taking a shower, Nia dried herself off, wrapped the

white towel around herself, and walked back to the bedroom. She reached inside her bag and pulled out her under wear and an over sized pink T-shirt with flowers imprinted on the front of it.

Nia put on her underwear and looked at herself in the mirror. She then started to brush her hair. It was very damp and very wavy in texture. She pulled her hair back and twisted it into a ball, securing it with a black bobby pin.

Nia plunged onto the bed and dialed her mom's phone number.

On the third ring, her mom answered the phone, "Hello."

"Hi, Mom, it's me," said Nia.

"Hi girl, your dad and I was waiting on your call. I see you made it safely."

"Yes, I did. Gosh Mom, you would really love California! It's so beautiful out here."

"Oh, really? Well I know I'll have to come visit you when you get yourself settled in. Well, I don't want to keep you, I don't want to run up your phone bill."

"OK, Mom, I love you and I'll talk to you later."

"I love you too, dear, and you take care of yourself. Call me back whenever you can. You can call us collect if you have to, because I want to hear from you."

"OK Mom, I'll talk to you later."

"OK, good night, Nia."

"Good night Mom." Nia hung up the phone.

It was still day time in California, but it was night time in New York; Nia knew it was going to take her a while to get adjusted to the time difference.

Nia watched some more TV. She drifted off to sleep with the remote control in her hand.

The very next day, which was Monday, Nia got up early. She went down the street to the grocery store, to get a newspaper. She wanted to look under the job classification ad. That same day, Nia went job hunting.

Two weeks has passed when Nia left the hotel and moved into a boarding house, because staying in the hotel was very expensive. Nia continued searching for jobs that fitted her work experience and training.

A month had passed since Nia arrived in California. She was both depressed and disappointed, she still haven't found a job. She was starting to get very worried; she didn't know how long her funds were going to last. When she first came to California, she had approximately $1500. And now, she already spent $1000.

Nia prayed every night for strength and guidance. She had to admit at times, she was beginning to lose faith, she became scared, and wanted to run back to New York to beg for her old job back. Nia knew that she could probably get her old job back in New York but something deep, down, inside her told her to keep on searching. In her heart she knew her blessings was just around the corner.

Chapter 15

Two months later, Nia got a job at a dental office. Nia had sold Clay's silver jeep for six thousand dollars before she came to California. With part of the money, she paid for her airplane ticket and living expenses until she found a job.

Nia was getting sick and tired of catching the bus to and from work, so with part of her first check and savings, Nia put a down payment on a new tan-colored 1991 Toyota Corolla. After a month of working at the dental office, Nia moved into a nice one-bedroom apartment.

While working at her new job, Nia met a friend, Asia Roberts. Asia showed Nia around the dental office and taught her the different procedures that would be part of Nia's job. Part of what Asia showed her was cleaning the dental equipment with bleach and other cleaners; Asia said that they cleaned their dental equipment between each patient due to the wide spread of the AIDS virus. A lot of people caught AIDS and other infections through unsanitary utensils used in dental offices across the nation.

Nia and Asia became instant friends. Asia was also a beautician. Asia talked Nia into getting her hair cut into a hair style.

On a Thursday evening, right after work, Nia went with Asia to her beauty shop, the Jazzy Touch Salon. At her booth, Asia took

Nia's hair down from it's pony tail and combed it. Nia's hair reached all the way down to her back.

"Girl, why on earth do you want a perm? You already have nice hair," said Asia.

"I just want something a little different," responded Nia.

"I think you only need a very mild relaxer, because you already have naturally soft wavy hair. But, Nia, aren't you afraid a relaxer will mess up your hair texture?" asked Asia putting on her gloves and parting Nia's hair.

"No, because I had a relaxer put in my hair before, and about a month later it turned back to it's natural grade," answered Nia.

"OK, I'll go on and put this relaxer in your hair," said Asia.

"Look through this *Black Hair Magazine* to decide on what hair style you want."

Asia left Nia to greet another customer. From across the room, Nia could hear Asia smacking and popping her bubble gum. A while back, Nia had asked her why she always chewed gum, and Asia said it was just a childhood habit. Asia went through two packs of bubble gum a day.

Asia was very pretty. Her skin was the color of caramel, and her eyes were slanted. Her skin and eyes reminded Nia of Asians, and that was also the reason why her mom had named her Asia. Asia and Nia wore the same size clothes, but Asia was taller than Nia; Asia was five feet six inches tall. She was also two years older than Nia. Asia's hair had it going on; it was cut very short, with lots of body and sheen.

Moments later, Nia heard Asia popping her gum close behind her.

"So Nia, have you decided on a style yet?"

Nia smiled at her and said, jokingly, "I want your hair style, Asia."

"I don't think so, girlfriend, because I know you! If I did that, you would have a fit, and I know I wouldn't hear the end of it," laughed Asia with her manicured finger nails raised in the air.

"But seriously, Asia, I like your hair style, it's real cute on you."

After Asia relaxed Nia's hair and washed the relaxer out with a neutralizer, she put a conditioner in her hair and then put her under the hair dryer. Nia flipped through a magazine until she found the perfect hair style. Nia showed Asia the hair style she wanted in the magazine.

"Oh girl, that is sharp!" exclaimed Asia. Asia looked at the hair style closely, and then cut Nia's hair precisely into the style. Nia's hair was cut into a long A-symmetric style. Her hair was still long in the back and flowed right down her back; Asia just trimmed the back of Nia's hair.

About an hour and a half later, Asia was finished with Nia's hair. Nia looked at herself in the mirror and smiled. Her hair felt softer and lighter on her head; it had so much body and sheen.

"Asia, you did a wonderful job with my hair, I'm glad you hooked me up." Nia admired her new hair do in the mirror.

"No problem girl, that's what friends are for, smiled Asia.

Chapter#16

Spring time 1991, filled the air of San Diego; the beach was alive with fun events. Asia's boyfriend, Keith, was originally from Los Angeles and he was the one who invited Asia. Keith told Asia that she could also bring a friend.

After work, Asia asked Nia if she wanted to go to a party.

"Sure, I would love to go," answered Nia.

"Well, I figured you probably wanted to go, especially since you said you wanted to see more of California."

"I'm glad you invited me. Oh, do you know what day it's going to be on?" asked Nia.

"Yep. Next Friday at 7:00 P.M.," replied Asia, taking off her latex gloves. She had just finished cleaning her last patient's teeth.

"Well, Girl, I guess I better go to the mall and buy me a bathing suit," said Nia.

"Nia, you mean to tell me you don't have a swim suit?" Asia asked in surprise.

"No, I don't. You know I'm from Brooklyn and never really been no place else. This is my first time ever leaving New York," said Nia as she cleaned the dental equipment.

"Well, I guess I'll go with you to help you pick out a swim-suit."

Nia was very excited about going to Los Angeles. Eventually, Friday rolled around, and after work, she went to Asia's house to get ready for the beach jam, in Los Angeles. After they changed clothes, they jumped into Asia's black Maxima and headed for the beach.

It was about 8:00 P.M. when they arrived. The beach party was supposed to be one of the biggest jams in the area. Most of the people there were college students who were on spring break. The party was live, and the music was jammin. All over the beach people in colorful swimsuits were moving to the beat. Asia and Nia got out of the car and walked towards the beach.

As usual, Asia's hair had it going on. This time, she had it highlighted in front, but still in the same Chinese bob style. Nia's hair was finger waved in front, while in the back, it hung straight and full. She loved her new hair style, and she kept thanking Asia for it.

Nia and Asia wanted to dress alike so under their cutoffs, they had on the same style bikinis, except Nia's was peach colored and Asia's was black. They both had on black L.A. Gears hiking boots and they knew they looked fly. Once they reached the beach, they received long flirtatious stares from the opposite sex.

Keith spotted Asia in the middle of the crowd. He yelled out her name loud enough to be heard across the crowded beach and blasting music.

"Asia!"

Asia thought she heard someone calling her, so she turned her head to try to see who it was.

Asia asked Nia, "Did you hear someone calling me?"

"Yes, I did. I believe that guy over there called you."

Nia pointed in the direction of the shout. Asia looked where Nia was pointing, and Asia spotted him. A smile came across her face when she saw him.

Asia waved her hands in the air and gestured for him to come over. Keith had to push, squeeze, and bo-guard his way through the crowd to reach Asia and Nia.

"Hi, Baby," smiled Keith.

Asia gave Keith a big hug.

"Hi, I've missed you."

Keith had a huge grin on his face.

"Really, Baby? I missed you too. When did you get here?" Keith gazed into Asia's eyes and studied her beautiful face.

"We just got here," replied Asia, holding his hands.

"Oh, did you bring Nia along?" asked Keith.

"Yes, Keith, I did and she's-" Asia turned around to introduce Nia to her boyfriend, only to discover she was gone.

With a confused look on her face, Asia asked Keith, "Now where did she go?"

"I don't know." Keith shrugged his shoulders.

"Well, she was just here a second ago," said Asia.

"Maybe I waved my magic wand and made her disappear. I'm glad she's gone; now I can have you all to myself," said Keith with a seductive smile. Keith held Asia in his strong arms and gently teased her ear.

"You naughty boy! We can do the booty later, but now I really want you to meet Nia," said Asia as she turned around and kissed him gently on the lips.

Later, Asia spotted Nia dancing with a guy wearing a blue starters shirt.

Asia touched Keith on his arm and said, "There she is."

After the song went off, Asia approached Nia.

"Girl, you left so quickly I didn't get a chance to introduce you to my boyfriend."

"Asia, I'm so sorry. This cute guy came up to me and asked me if I wanted to dance. I started to tell you but you was talking to Keith, and I didn't want to disturb you, so I figured I would go dance with this cute brother for one song and then come back to where you all were," said Nia, going on and on with her explanation.

"That's OK, Nia, I accept your apology. But anyway, this is Keith, and Keith, this is Nia."

"I'm pleased to meet you," said Nia.

Keith nodded his head," The same."

Moments later, Asia's favorite song, "Too Legit to Quite," by M.C.Hammer was being played by the D.J.

"Girl, this is my song; I gots to dance to this one," said Asia. Asia left Nia and went back into the crowd to dance with Keith.

Nia was hot and thirsty so she went to the refreshment table to get some punch. While at the table sipping on her tropical punch, she suddenly spotted him. Nia could not take her eyes off him. He was tall, about six foot three inches, with the prettiest chocolate colored skin she had ever seen. From the distance, he was what you would call a true stud; his body was rippling with muscles. He had on a tank top that showed off his tantalizing, strong, muscular biceps.

While sipping on her punch, another song came on. The song was "Poison" by BBD (Bell, Biv, Duvoe). "Poison was one of Nia's personal favorites. She hurried and finished drinking her punch and went back into the crowd.

Meanwhile, little did Nia realize that the attractive man that she was staring at earlier was looking at her and admiring her beauty. He watched her for a while and then headed in her direction and started dancing right behind her. Nia knew that some guy was bumpin and grindin close behind her, but she didn't pay it no mind because she knew that was how some guys dance with girls and she considered it down right freaky and nasty.

Finally Nia turned around and kept on dancing to the beat. Nia looked up and realized that it was the same man she had been staring at.

After realizing that she was dancing with this hunk of a man, Nia was spellbound. She smiled at him in a very flirtatious manner and he smiled back. Nia noticed that he had a nice smile; his teeth were pretty, straight, and pearly white.

Suddenly, a slow jam came on, "Uhh Ahh" by Boyz II Men. The mysterious man asked her, "May I have this dance?"

"Sure," she answered.

He slipped his strong arms around her small waist in a very warm embrace. They slowly danced to the rhythm of the song. Nia looked up at him again and they both made eye contact. His eyes was so beautiful, dark brown and shiny. They seemed to sparkle just like the stars in the sky.

Nia gently laid her head on his shoulder. It felt so good to dance close to him and to be in his arms. In a strange way, Nia felt comfortable with him; usually she didn't feel this way about men. Nia was quite impressed, because not only did he look good but he smelled good, too. He was wearing "Eternity," one of the fragrances Nia loved to smell on men.

After the song ended, the D.J. played Naughty By Nature's song called "Hip Hop Hurray". The gorgeous man took Nia's hands into his strong hands and lead her from the crowd.

When they finally moved away from the crowd and loud music, he said, "Well I didn't have a chance to formally introduce myself. My name is Derick Carter, and most people just call me Black, it's my nick name. What's your name, by the way?"

"My name is Nia Chevez."

Black slowly eyed her up and down before saying, "Well Nia, that's a beautiful name for a fine sister like yourself." All Nia could do was blush at his compliment.

"Nia, do you mind if we go for a walk along the beach and talk for a while?"

Nia was a bit hesitant for a second. She usually didn't go anywhere with strangers, but for some reason, she felt like she could trust him.

"I'm not going to bite," said Black as if reading her mind.

"Sure, I would love to."

While walking and looking at the beautiful scenery, Nia and Black continued their conversation.

"So Nia, are you from California?"

"No, I'm from Brooklyn, New York. Where are you from?" asked Nia, smiling and looking up at him.

"Oh, I'm from Detroit, Michigan."

Black continued, "I first came to San Diego when I was in the military three years ago...I thought California was so beautiful, I've been here ever since."

For about an hour and a half, Nia and Black talked to each other and enjoyed each other's company while walking and finally sitting on a big rock which over looked the shore.

The beach was beautiful, with a clear sky and the moon and stars shining brightly. The ocean's waves gently swept across the sandy beach. And the wind blew gracefully against the palm trees, causing them to sway softly from side to side.

Black said, "You know what?"

"What?"

"When I first saw you, I thought you were the most beautiful woman I have ever seen. Your hair is so pretty, and your skin looks so soft," said Black and with that, he lifted his hands and gently caressed her soft cheeks. Nia blushed at his compliments, and she felt a burst of energy when he caressed her skin.

Black continued to look at her and asked, "Are you mixed with something?"

"Yes, I'm half black and half Hispanic. Why did you ask me that?"

"Because of your light skin and your hair texture," answered Black. Black and Nia looked at each other in a brief moment of mutual attraction.

He glanced down at her breasts. Quickly he looked back into her eyes and saw that she had some pretty eyes. He was not only attracted to her physically, but he also enjoyed her company. Black knew then that he wanted her phone number so he could keep in contact with her.

Later, Asia and Keith came over to where Nia and Black were on the beach. Asia yelled, "Nia!"

Nia turned around and saw that it was Asia. She got up and walked towards Asia and Keith.

Asia said, "Nia, I'm about ready to go because it's going on 12:00, and we both have to go to work in the morning."

"OK, Asia. Asia, can you wait one second, I just want to say goodbye to this guy."

"OK, I'll meet you at the car."

Asia and Keith walked away holding hands.

Nia turned around and ran towards Black. Black watched her as she ran. He was so captivated by her beauty. The gentle wind blew Nia's long beautiful hair back from her face. Her lovely breasts were bouncing as she ran towards him.

Finally Nia reached him.

"Black, I'm sorry, but I have to go."

"OK, but Nia before you go, can I have your phone number?"

"Sure, of course, you can have my number."

Both of them exchanged numbers. Nia and Black walked together toward Asia's car. They continued to talk and laughed together.

When they reached Asia's car, Asia and Keith were already there. Asia hugged and passionately kissed Keith goodbye.

Nia smiled at Black and said, "Goodbye."

"I'll call you sometime tomorrow."

"OK," said Nia as she got in the car.

After getting settled in the car, she and Asia took off into the night in the black Nissan Maxima.

Chapter 17

The next day, Black called Nia. They enjoyed talking to each other so much that they stayed on the phone for two straight hours.

"How would you like it if we were to go out sometimes?"

"Sure, Black, I would love to."

"How about tomorrow afternoon at 4:00?" asked Black.

"OK."

Nia gave Black the address to her apartment complex.

"I guess tomorrow it is. I'll see you then," said Black.

"OK, I'll talk to you later."

They both said goodbye to each other and hung up the phone.

Right after Nia got off the phone, she yelled, "Yes, yes, yes!" And then she started jumping up and down with joy. She was so thrilled that he had actually asked her out.

"Oh my gosh, what am I going to wear?" thought Nia aloud.

The next day was Saturday. While Nia was getting ready to go out, Asia came over to see what Nia was going to wear. Asia was just as excited as Nia. She was glad that her home girl was finally going out on a date.

Nia decided to wear her black bodysuit with an over-sized royal blue v-necked sweater. With her outfit, she wore a pair of black flats with a black purse to match. Asia did Nia's hair in a sharp, long straight style with lots of body and sheen.

As Nia looked at herself in the mirror, she was pleased with what she saw. Nia knew that she had it going on.

At 4:00, Blacked arrived and took Nia to a steak and grill restaurant. Before they reached the restaurant, Black took her for a spin in his brand new red Camaro. While they walked toward the car, Nia noticed that the tag on the front of the vehicle read, "2 Hot 2 Handle."

"Does '2 Hot 2 Handle' represent you or the car?"

"I'll just leave that up to you to decide," and with that, he gave her a wink.

Nia smiled at his remark. As a perfect gentleman, he opened the door for her and Nia got in.

So far, Nia was quite impressed with this man. This evening she noticed that he looked even more handsome than he did at the beach. The brother was fine, she thought.

In the restaurant, Nia finally had a chance to take a good look at Black. He was well dressed in a navy blue Nike sweatsuit and a pair of black leather Air Jordan high tops. His dark skin was smooth and seemed to be glistering. His mustache and goatee were neatly trimmed; his hair was neatly cut in a low box. When Nia looked at his fingernails at the dinner table, she noticed that his nails were short and clean.

While eating and conversing with Black, she learned that he owned his own computer repair shop. His company sold small parts to large corporations for their computers. He told her that they did repairs on computers and maintained services for large corporations that he had under contract.

Black had two houses, two cars, and a truck. Besides his Camaro, he had a gray BMW, and a blue Ford pick up truck to carry his supplies and parts for his business.

Leaving the restaurant, Nia had a big smile on her face. Gosh, I am having a wonderful time! I hope he feels the same way too, she thought.

Nia looked at him and saw that his eyes were glued to the road as he drove.

"What are you thinking about?" curiously asked Nia.

"I've been thinking about what a wonderful time I'm having with you."

Hearing those words, made her feel good inside.

"Nia, I've noticed something about you."

"What have you noticed about me?" asked Nia, as she leaned back in her seat.

"Well, I've noticed that you have said very little about yourself."

"Well, Black, there is not much to talk about. But if you want to know something about me I'll tell you. I'm from Brooklyn, New York. Both of my parents are deceased. The Thompsons adopted me and raised me as part of their family. And I'm a dental hygienist at a dental office."

"Oh, and you think that's a lot about yourself, because in one night you know practically everything about me. I've talked about my relatives, friends, school, my business, the military, and even some of my past relationships," chuckled Black, still watching the road as he drove.

Black glanced at Nia.

"It's like you're a mystery, as if you are hiding something, Nia," said Black as he gazed at her with piercing eyes.

Nia didn't like where this conversation was heading. It was like he could hear her mind and thoughts. I know I haven't told him much about myself, she thought. I love being with Black, but it is just too soon to tell him about my deep dark past.

"I'm not trying to hide anything, Black. I don't like leaking all my business to people, especially when I'm trying to get to know them. It takes time for me to warm up to people," said Nia.

"Yeah right, Nia. I know a sweet fine thang like you can practically get any man you want." added Black.

"Black, I'm not being secretive. I just don't like to talk about my past much."

Nia was becoming a little hostile. From her facial expression, Black knew that he was not going to get anywhere with this conversation, but he just couldn't help wanting to know. He was so curious about what she had to hide. He had the impression that whatever her past was, it really upset her a lot to talk about it. Black decided to let it go; he figured that eventually, she would open up to him.

For a moment, there was nothing but complete silence. Black wanted to break the silence, so he spoke.

"Nia, I know you'll like Santa Monica. It is very beautiful."

"I hope it is as beautiful as most people say it is," said Nia.

Gradually, the conversation flowed smoothly again between Nia and Black.

Finally, they arrived. Nia was intrigued with the beauty of Santa Monica. The scenery of the beach was spectacular. As they looked out into the ocean, the sun seemed to meet the open waters. The beach was a beautiful golden bronze, and the palm trees gracefully danced along to the music of the gentle breeze.

Always the gentleman, Black walked around to the passenger side of the car to open the door for her. After leaving the car, they walked along the beach.

While walking along the beach and enjoying the lovely sunset,

Black held Nia in his strong arms. His embrace felt so warm and sincere that she rested her head against his solid chest.

Nia even liked it when he ran his fingers gently through her hair.

"Nia, you have some pretty hair. It is so shiny and soft," whispered Black.

He gently swept Nia's hair so that it rested on the other side of her shoulder. Along her neck, he created a trail of sweet wet kisses. Nia laughed at first because it tickled but after a while, it was starting to feel real good. Those soft gentle wet kisses were starting to turn Nia on. All of sudden she felt a surge of energy.

"Black, I think you should stop doing that."

"OK," grinned Black.

Black could tell that she enjoyed the kisses he planted on her neck.

After the romantic walk along the beach, Black drove Nia home. He walked her up to her apartment door.

"Well, Nia, I guess this is it."

"Yeah, I had a wonderful time," smiled Nia.

Nia started to turned her key in the door, but Black touched her shoulder.

"Nia, do you think I will have a chance to see you again?"

"Why of course," answered Nia as she looked up at him.

They shared a moment of eye contact. Black moved closer to her and wrapped his arms around her small waist. He looked down at her, and then he tilted his head and placed a soft, gentle kiss upon Nia's lips.

"Good night, Black."

"Good night, Nia, and I'll call you later."

After the date, Nia took off her clothes and took a shower.

Once she got comfortable in her pajamas, she had a strong craving for something sweet to eat. She went to the kitchen and got some choco-late chip cookies and poured herself a glass of milk. With her food in her hand, she walked to the sofa and sat down. Thinking about her wonderful evening. Nia couldn't wait to tell Asia about the date, but she couldn't call her because she was out with Keith.

Nia was bored just sitting there munching on her cookies, so she turned on the t.v. with the remote control. She flipped through the channels, and there was nothing good on, so she clicked off the t.v. with disappointment. She decided to call her mom to see how she was doing. Nia hadn't heard from her mom in a while, and she missed her deeply. Nia picked up the phone and dialed her mom's number.

The phone rang three times before little Joseph answered the phone. Nia had to stop thinking of him as a little boy, because Joseph was now fifteen years old, going on sixteen. Joseph was a young man now, looking forward to getting his drivers' license.

"Hello," answered Joseph in his newly defined masculine voice.

"Hi Joseph, it's me, Nia."

"What's up! How is it going in California?" asked Joseph. He was happy to hear from his other big sister.

"Oh, it's great, Joseph, you would really love it here!"

"I imagine so with the beautiful weather and all those fine babes in bikinis."

"Boy, you're crazy, you'd love to go anywhere where there are girls who are half dressed," laughed Nia.

"Did you want to talk to Mom?" asked Joseph.

"Yeah, put her on the phone, please," answered Nia.

"OK, just wait a second. I have to get this other person off the other line," said Joseph.

Joseph put Nia on hold for a second and then clicked back over to her line.

"Hello?"

"Hello?" replied Nia.

"Mom, telephone! It's Nia!" shouted Joseph.

A moment later, Mrs. Thompson answered the phone, "Hello?"

"Hi mom, how are you doing?" asked Nia.

"Oh, I'm doing fine. How are things in California?" asked Mrs. Thompson.

"Oh just fine, now that I'm finally settled in. Guess what, Mom? I just bought me a new car."

"Nia, that's wonderful! So when can I fly out there to see you?"

"Oh, Mom, anytime, you know you are always welcome here," replied Nia.

"Well, I guess I can go on ahead and start planning to spend a week with you in California."

"Oh that sounds so great, Mom!" exclaimed Nia. She was really looking forward to seeing her mom again.

"Mom, how is Dad?"

"Oh, he's fine. He's still working as hard as usual," she answered.

"How is Charlene?" asked Nia.

Nia hadn't heard from Charlene in a long time.

"Oh, she's fine. I'm glad she broke up with that no good boyfriend of hers," mumbled Mom.

"You mean to tell me that she broke up with Doug?" asked Nia, surprisingly.

"Yes," answered Mrs. Thompson.

"But I thought they were getting married."

"No, they're not and I'm glad they're not," added Mrs. Thompson with delight.

"Mom, why do you despise Doug so much?"

"I just didn't like how he treated her. He spoke to her any kind of way and was always asking her for money when he made more than she did. Doug knew that Charlene was struggling financially and was trying to finish college, but it just seemed like he was trying to keep her from graduating. I'm so glad that she's focusing on her education, now. I'm hoping she'll graduate by next fall."

"What made Charlene break up with him?" asked Nia, taking another bite into her cookie.

"She caught him in bed with another woman."

"No way, Mama, how could that be!"

"Well it happened, and I'm glad she left that no good bastard!"

"Well, where is she staying?" asked Nia.

"She moved out from him and moved back home with us until she gets herself together".

"Dang, I hate that happened to her," uttered Nia.

"Yeah, me too. I just wish she would have listened to me in the first place, when I told her not move in with that no good nigga," added Mama.

"Maybe she learned from this and won't make the same mistake twice," sighed Nia.

"I hope so. It just makes me so angry when any man thinks he can run over a woman and treat her any kind of way, especially when it comes to my daughters. When you all hurt, I hurt also, because you all are so dear to me."

"Mama, there's something I want to tell you."

"What's that, dear?"

"I wanted to tell you I'm dating this guy name Black."

"Black? What kind of name is that!"

"Mom, that's his nickname; his real name is Derrick. He owns a business just like Daddy, and he seems to be a very nice guy. I would like for you to meet him one day," said Nia.

"I would like to meet him, too, dear. Well, I don't want to run up your phone bill."

"OK, Mom, I'll talk to you later. You do have my new phone number, don't you?" questioned Nia.

"Yes, I do, and I'll give you a ring to check up on you," answered Mrs. Thompson.

"OK, good night, Mom. I love you."

"I love you, too. I'll talk to you later."

On Wednesday, Nia and Black planned on going out together on Friday and finally, Friday rolled around. Black arrived right on time for the date. Nia knew she had it going; she knew that she was dressed to kill. Wanting to look extra fine, Nia had on a short, tight, black spandex dress. The front part of the dress was very low cut, and it showed off her cleavage. Nia also had on a pair of black high heel shoes which matched her dress perfectly.

Nia was putting on her gold ear rings when Black rang the doorbell. Once Nia heard the bell, she rushed to the door to answer it.

When she opened the door, Black smiled and said, "Hello." Nia liked what she saw. Black looked gorgeous in his black Armani suit.

Black took a good look at Nia and was totally mesmorized. Damn, home girl is fine, he thought.

Nia invited Black in.

"Black, can you wait a second, I need to get my purse?"

"Sure," responded Black.

As Nia walked away, he took another good look at her. All he could do was shake his head because, not only did she have a beautiful face, but she also had a great body; Black was very attracted to her. He knew that all evening it was going to be hard to keep his eyes off her.

I know other men are going to be looking at her, too, but I'm going to put my arms around her to show them that she is with me, he thought. Maybe I shouldn't be so possessive of her, she's not even my girlfriend yet, thought Black. She may not be mine now, but soon she will be, he thought; and with that thought a devilish grin came across his face.

Nia finally returned from her bedroom.

Black looked around at her apartment and said, "Nia, this is a nice place you have here."

"Why, thank you," smiled Nia.

Black noticed her cute smile.

Nia and Black headed straight to the French restaurant. Once they got there, Nia was very impressed; the restaurant actually had valet parking. This was Nia's first time going to such an expensive and fancy restaurant. Black watched Nia's eyes sparkle, and it made him chuckle. He knew that Nia came from the projects and slum area of Brooklyn, New York. He also knew that she has never been in such an extravagant setting; he liked watching the surprised look on her face.

Once they went inside the restaurant, Nia noticed how fancy everything was: expensive silverware and elegant fine china, tables with beautifully lit candles. There was also a violinist playing romantic music for a couple; oh how romantic she thought!

Gosh, can he really afford all of this? she wondered. Well, I guess he can afford this, because if he couldn't, he wouldn't have brought me here, she thought.

Moments later, a hostess lead them to their reserved table.

"So, how do you like it?" asked Black.

"This seems like a wonderful restaurant, and the food smells so good."

"Well, Nia, I just wanted to take you somewhere nice."

"Black, you have done a great job of choosing a nice restaurant," said Nia as she beamed at him from across the table.

Nia looked around the restaurant and noticed that they were the only blacks.

"Black, did you know we're the only black people in this joint?"

Black leaned back in his chair and laughed because he thought that her remark was funny.

"Black, what's so funny?"

"I was laughing because I saw you looking around, and I just knew that you were going to mention that."

"Nia, a lot of rich upper class people come to this restaurant. African Americans don't come to this restaurant often, because either they feel uncomfortable about being the only black in here, or either they can't afford it. I personally come here because of my personal theory."

"And what's your theory, Black?"

"My theory is that if I can afford something nice every once in a while, why not go and get it? Nobody is going to stop me from going to places that I enjoy, especially racist mother fuckers, because they can all kiss my black ass."

While observing the restaurant, Nia noticed that they were sitting near a window, and outside the window, was a lovely view of the ocean. The strong waves of the sea were crashing against the huge rocks. In the sky, the moon was shining brightly and the stars were twinkling.

Black watched Nia from across the table. During their quiet moment, Black looked at her while she was staring out the window. Black realized that Nia was such an attractive woman; she was so beautiful that often he found it hard to take his eyes off her. She was definitely a wonderful sight to see, he thought.

From across the table, he noticed her lovely, soft, caramel colored skin. Her long, straight, silky, black hair flowed gracefully down her shoulders. He noticed her prominent features, like high cheek bones and soft full lips.

He began to wonder what it would be like to kiss them in a more passionate manner. Her eyes were such a pretty brown color with a touch of innocence, which reminded him of Bambi. But behind those beautiful, big, brown eyes, there was also a mystery of the painful past that he so eagerly wanted to know about.

Black's eyes lowered down toward her breasts. Through her dress, he could see her cleavage. Her breasts were a nice size, they looked like they were more than a hand full. His mind drifted to sexual desires. He daydreamed about what it would be like to make wild passionate love to her.

Black's thoughts were interrupted when the waiter approached them. "Have you both decided on what you want to order for dinner?"

Nia glanced down at her menu and didn't have a clue as to what to order, all of the food on the menu was foreign to her. From the expression on her face, Black knew she didn't know what to order, so he ordered for her.

Nia was quite impressed that he knew French. After Black gave the waiter their order, the waiter picked up the menus and walked away.

"What did you order for me, Black?"

"Oh, I just ordered some snails," replied Black with a stern look on his face. Nia looked at him and couldn't tell if he was serious or not.

"No, seriously, what did you order for me?"

"I said snails," he answered, his facial expression still didn't change.

"Well, what if I don't like snails?"

"Then I would order you something else."

"And what would that something else be?"

"Octopus!" laughed Black.

"Gosh, girl, you ask a lot of questions."

"Did you really think I ordered snails for you?"

"Yeah, because you looked like you was for real." Nia laughed with him because she knew that he had her actually believing him.

"Black, you're good at fooling people, but I'll get you next time."

"Well, I don't know if you can fool me because I'm the master."

Nia watched Black while he was smiling at her. Gosh he's a very handsome man, she thought. His body is out of this world. She admired his long thick eyelashes his lovely dark skin, his teeth were straight and so white they actually gleamed.

The waiter returned with cheese fondue with apple and bread, salad, champagne, and ice tea.

Black watched Nia as she ate her food. She ate like a bird; somehow, that didn't surprise him because she was so petite. He figured that she probably weighed no more than 120 pounds.

Compared to him, she was very short; she barely reached his shoulder.

Black was hungry, so he dug right in.

Within ten minutes, he had finished most of all of his appetizer and salad.

"Man, I finished eating all my food. Now I'm ready for the real deal. Damn, girl, you still eating on that salad, you eat like a bird!" exclaimed Black.

Fifteen minutes later, the waiter returned with their meal. Black had ordered marinated chicken cooked with fresh vegetables sautéed in white wine. He ordered the same meal for the both of them.

"Um, um, um, Black, this is delicious!"

"You like it?"

"Yes, I really do! We should come back to this restaurant again some day."

While they ate, they continued to converse with each another. Black talked about himself mostly, but the conversation was very interesting to Nia. She was intrigued by what he had to say.

"Black, you have such an interesting life. You have accomplished so much for a young man. How old are you?" asked Nia.

"Oh, I'm thirty."

"Really? I bet your mom is very proud of you."

"Yeah, she is," smiled Black.

"Nia, there's something else I've been wanting to tell you."

"What is it, Black?"

"I was married once, but we divorced about three years ago."

"Oh, really? How long were you married?" Nia put down her champagne glass to listen closely.

"We were married for two years."

"May I ask why you got a divorce?"

"Sure, I want to be open and honest with you, Nia. My ex-wife divorced me because of my drinking problem. That was a long time ago, and now I'm clean."

Black looked at his glass of tea and then at Nia.

"I haven't had any alcohol in three years," he added.

Nia glanced at his glass and realized that he was drinking ice tea.

After dinner, they went to a jazz club. As soon as they strolled into the club, Nia received a lot of stares from men. Black noticed the stares and placed his arm around her waist to show that she was with him.

Inside the club, there was a crowd already on the dance floor. The music was soft with a smooth melody. Once on the dance floor, they started dancing in each others' arms to the sweet sound of the jazz band.

Two different guys asked to cut in to dance with Nia. Black was cool with the first guy, but when the second guy asked to cut in, Black began to get irritated. He felt very jealous seeing Nia dancing with other people other than himself.

When Nia had finished dancing with the second guy, Black walked up to her and took her by the hand; he held her hand in such a firm grip that it hurt her. When they got to the table, he pulled her chair out for her and then went to his side to sit down. From his expression, Nia could tell that he was upset and very jealous. She liked that in a way because it showed her that he had strong feelings for her.

At 12:30, Nia and Black left the club. Once they got in the car, Black admitted to Nia that he did get a little bit jealous watching her dance with other men.

After a twenty minute drive from the club, they reached Nia's apartment. Black got out of the car and walked her to the door

Once she opened the door, she turned around and asked, "Do you want to come inside and have something to drink?"

"Sure, I would like that."

Black was glad that she asked him in, because he really didn't feel like leaving yet. He loved Nia's company and wanted to talk to her some more.

Black walked in behind her and locked the door.

"Make yourself right at home. Have a seat on the couch," said Nia as she went to her bedroom to take off her high heel.

Black sat down on the couch and got comfortable.

Black looked around the apartment. Nia's living room was very warm, soft, and feminine, he thought. She had an emerald green leather sofa, love seat, and chair. Black looked down at the glass coffee table and noticed Nia's small porcelain unicorn figurines. What a collection, he thought. Underneath her coffee table was a beautiful oriental styled-rug that blended well with her furnishings.

On the wall, Black noticed some pictures. The one that really captured his attention was a black and white military picture of a Hispanic man. Maybe that's her father, he thought, because he could see a resemblance between him and Nia. She had his eyes, strong jaw, and high cheek bones. Next to the picture was a photograph of a little girl with pigtails hugging an old Mexican woman. And there was also a picture that sat on top of Nia's bookshelf; the picture was a photo of a beautiful light skinned woman wearing a floral sun dress.

"I hope you don't mind me taking off my shoes, but those heels were killing my feet," smiled Nia as she nestled into the sofa next to Black.

"I see you like unicorns." said Black while pointing to her figurines with a grin on his face.

"Yeah, I have always loved unicorns ever since I was a little girl."

"I've been looking at the pictures on your wall, and the one that really caught my eye is the guy in the military uniform," said Black looking at the picture.

"Oh, yeah, that's my father. His name was Carlos Chevez."

"How did he die?" Black recalled her mentioning that both her parents were deceased.

Black turned around to look at Nia, and then he rested his elbow on the back of the sofa.

Nia looked at him and said, "Well, he died in combat during the Vietnam War. I never had a chance to meet him, because he died right before I was born."

"Gosh, Nia, I'm sorry to hear that."

"You know, a lot of times, I've wished that he had never died. As a kid, I used to imagine and dream about what my father would have been like if he was still alive."

"Did your mother ever talk about how your father was as a person?"

"Oh yes, quite often, as a matter of fact. She told me that he had a great sense of humor and always had people rolling over laughing at his jokes. She told me he was very strong, smart, warm-hearted, and had such a well rounded beautiful personality, which was why she fell in love with him."

"Gosh, he sounds like he was a real good man," said Black, listening to every word Nia was telling him.

Nia got up from the couch. "Do you want something to drink?"

"Yeah, what do you have?"

"I have some Coca Cola, grape Kool Aid, and Sprite."

"I'll have me a Sprite," replied Black.

"OK," said Nia as she went to the kitchen.

Nia opened the refrigerator, grabbed two cans of Sprite, went back to the living room, and sat next to Black.

"Who is the elderly woman with the little girl?" asked Black, still looking at the pictures.

"Oh that's me and Grandma Maria. She was the one who helped my mom raise me until I turned nine years old. And the woman in the flowered dress is my mother."

Black watched Nia as she spoke. He was so intrigued with her rich family history. He was happy that she was finally opening up to him.

Black and Nia looked into each others' eyes and then leaned over to each other to kiss. Their lips met into a sweet innocent kiss; Black moved closer to Nia so he could place his arms around her small waist. He lifted his right hand up and ran his fingertips through her dark silky hair. Their kiss turned from an innocent spark into fiery flames of passion.

They were captured by the heat of the moment, and one thing lead into another. Nia's heart was beating fast; she knew she wanted Black. Black's hands moved down to her thigh and on up to her breasts; he gently caressed them as he continued to kiss her soft sweet lips.

His wet kisses moved from her lips to her chin and on down to her neck. Nia tilted her head back and closed her eyes as she enjoyed the touch of his soft lips and tongue against her warm skin. His kisses moved closer and closer to her swollen breasts, but he stopped right before he reached them. Nia stuck out her chest in hope that he would rub and caress her breasts, but instead his kisses moved back up her neck and then to her ear. He started to kiss and gently nuzzle her ear with his lips and tongue.

He whispered in her ear, "Nia, I really want you tonight," in a deep lustful voice. Nia was so wet between her legs. She wanted him badly, too.

Nia looked at Black and said softly, "I want you, too."

They got up from the couch. Nia took his hands and led him to her bedroom.

Black sat down on the soft queen size bed, and Nia stood before him. Slowly, Nia pulled off her dress and stood there wearing only her black lace lingerie. Black watched her every move. Her honey colored skin glistened. Nia had on a pair of thong lace panties. Black's hands moved up and he gently rubbed her butt.

Watching Nia undress before him was very arousing, he felt himself get rock hard. Nia unhooked her bra strap and took off her bra. Black's eyes stared right at her beautifully well-endowed breasts. Nia pulled out a chair and placed her foot on it as she rolled down her silk black stocking. Then she switched legs and did the same with the other stocking. She took off her garter belt and panties.

Nia stood before Black with no clothes on. Black looked at her with lust, and drops of perspiration came rolling down his forehead. Nia sat on the bed beside him.

Black quickly took off his clothes as if he was running in a marathon race. After he took off his clothes, he stood before Nia nude. His body was very lean, but solid. His abdomen was nothing but waves of muscle, and his legs were well proportionate to his upper body. On his chest, there was not a strand of hair. Nia looked up at his handsome face.

He sat beside Nia and placed his arms around her. Nia looked down and he was huge; she was afraid that it was going to hurt.

He whispered, "Don't worry, it won't be painful. I'll be gentle," as if to read her mind.

"Wait a sec, let me get a condom out of my wallet."

Later, Black started kissing Nia and caressing her gently on all the right parts of her body. Nia was breathless when Black went down and ate her out; it was so new to her that it thrilled her into an orgasm.

After foreplay, Black gently entered her and moved to the beat of an African drum. Nia winced in pain as he entered her, but after she loosened up, she felt lots of pleasure. After the spellbinding experience of making love, both of them were exhausted. Black held Nia in his arms, and they talked for a while. Later that night, they drifted off into a deep sleep.

The next morning, Nia woke up and discovered that Black was not by her side. She sat up and fear came over her. Nia started to feel hurt; she hoped that Black was not a dog who had left her after having a good fuck. She got up from the bed; her heart was beating real fast. The aroma of food coming from the kitchen suddenly brought a smile to her face.

Nia put on an oversized T-shirt and walked into the kitchen. Black was whipping up a hearty breakfast.

"I thought I'd fix my beautiful princess breakfast," said Black with a grin on his face.

Nia smiled back at him and said, "I'm glad you're still here. When I woke up this morning and saw that you was not laying beside me, I was afraid that you left."

"Now, how could I leave someone as special as you?"

Nia blushed at his sweet remark and stood behind him; she wrapped her arms around his waist and hugged him real tight. She stood on tiptoe to plant a kiss on his cheek and later rested her head on his back.

"What's that for?" he asked right after she kissed him.

"That's for being so kind and so sweet," replied Nia.

Black smiled and turned around to face her.

"Why was you afraid that I left you?" curiously asked Black.

"I was afraid that you only wanted to be with me last night because you only wanted to have sex with me. I don't want you to think that I'm easy, because I slept with you so fast. We only met about two weeks ago," said Nia looking up at him.

Black looked at Nia and was again amazed at how attractive she was, even after just waking up . Nia was so sweet and soft; she reminded him of a baby.

"Come here, Baby. I'm not like that. I really do like you and care about you. You're really starting to grow on me, and I'll always be here for you as a friend, regardless of what happens in our relationship," said Black as he held her in his arms.

Nia gently laid her head against his strong chest. She knew that it was definitely the start of a higher level in their relationship; she knew that she was falling in love with him. Nia just hoped that he felt the same way, too.

Chapter #18

Right after Black left Nia's apartment, Nia changed clothes and got ready to go over to Asia's house. She couldn't wait to tell Asia about her wonderful date with Black. Nia hopped into her Toyota and zoomed over to Asia's place.

Nia rung the doorbell, and Asia answered it.

"Hi, girl, how are you doing? Come on in," said Asia.

"Oh, I'm doing fine," replied Nia as she walked through the door.

Nia sat down on Asia's sofa. Asia lived in a gorgeous condo. In the middle of the living room, a stunning hand-woven rug covered a portion of the polished wooden floor. Over the fireplace, Asia had hung a huge picture of herself in a bikini.

"Dang, Asia, that's a pretty picture of you! When did you have it taken?"

"Oh, about three years ago. I was walking along the beach one day, and this photographer asked me if he could take a picture of me. I told him sure, so I posed for him. He told me to come by the shop later on during the week to take a look at the pictures. When I went by the shop and saw the pictures, I thought they were lovely, so he gave me this framed picture to keep."

"So, Asia, what's been going on?" asked Nia.

"Oh, nothing much. Last night Keith and I went to the movies and ate some Chinese food," said Asia as she sat next to Nia

"Girlfriend, I want to hear about your date with Black," said Asia with a huge smile on her face.

Nia laughed and told Asia about the date.

"Well, I had a wonderful time. We went out to this real expensive French restaurant and, after that, he took me to this nice jazz club, right on Bruce Street. We both had a good time dancing the whole night away," beamed Nia as she reminisced about the night before.

"Ooh, girl, it sounds like you did have a great time!" exclaimed Asia.

Asia was so happy for Nia. She wanted Nia to find a good man who would treat her right.

"And, girl, not only that, he even came to my apartment, and we talked for hours about a lot of things. We also did the do," said Nia.

"What do you mean you 'did the do'?" asked Asia.

She was not catching on to what Nia was saying.

"You know, we did the do," repeated Nia.

"Oh really! Was he good?" asked Asia.

Asia had finally caught on to what Nia was saying.

"He was wonderful. He was more than I ever anticipated." answered Nia, in a daze.

"Oh, girl, that's great!" exclaimed Asia.

"And, girl, not only was he good in the bedroom, but he can also throw down in the kitchen! Brother man can show nuf cook some good food!" exclaimed Nia.

"Damn, girl! He sounds like he's a real good catch."

"Yeah I hope so," said Nia.

Nia stayed at Asia's house for a while longer and then she left to go home. While driving home, Nia had a lot on her mind. She hoped that she wasn't moving too fast in this relationship. She didn't want to end up getting hurt in the long run. Nia knew that her feelings for Black was growing more and more each day.

One evening at Black's house, Nia and Black had rented a movie and were watching it over a bag of microwave popcorn.

After the movie was over, Black got up to rewind the video tape.

"That was a pretty good movie, wasn't it?" asked Black.

"Yeah, but it had a sad ending," said Nia as she stood up and stretched.

"Yeah, it did have a sad ending. I saw you crying over there," said Black with a grin.

"Having one of the favorite main characters die near the end made me cry," said Nia.

"You're just very emotional." said Black as he took the video tape out of the VCR and placed it inside the box.

"Nia, will you remind me to take this movie back? You know that I can be very forgetful at times."

"OK," replied Nia.

Nia loved going over to Black's house. It was a long, low, ranch style house, trimmed in antique brick. His taste in furniture was very manly. The living room had a country touch to it; on the wall, was a bold oil painting of a black buffalo soldier galloping on his horse. Over the gray and blue colored sofa, there was a wooden ceiling fan.

In Black's dining room, he had a beautiful glass table trimmed in black and gold; there were six chairs that matched the table. Black's bedroom was black and white. In one of the bathrooms there was a garden tub, which felt just as good as a Jacuzzi, except it's not as large as a Jacuzzi; his bathroom was burgundy in color.

Nia's favorite room in Black's house was the sun room; it featured a sunroof, making it the brightest room in the house. Nia loved to go in this room at night and look up at the stars and the moon because it was so beautiful. To her, this was the most peaceful room in the house. The room was also filled with all sorts of wonderful paintings. Nia could tell that Black was really into fine arts.

"Black, you have such a beautiful house," said Nia, thinking about how nice his home looked.

"Oh thank you, " said Black modestly.

Black sat next to Nia and took her small hands in his.

"Nia, there's something I've been intending to ask you."

"Yes, what is it?" asked Nia, looking at him.

Their eyes met. Nia stared into his dark quartz like eyes.

"Well, Nia, I've been thinking that since I met you, I've been so much happier. It's like you're my sunshine, you just brighten up my spirits every time I'm with you. Nia I want you to move in with me after your lease is up on your apartment. I know it is quite soon, but I really do believe that it would work out well for both of us."

"Well, Black, it is quite sudden, but I'll think about it and let you know. Nia was quite shocked by what he asked her; a part of her said yes but another part of her said no. Nia knew that this would be a very big step in their relationship.

"Your lease is not up until November, so you have two months to think about it. I just want you to consider it," added Black.

Black didn't mention it again that night nor for the rest of the month. He didn't want to push or pressure her into anything.

Two months passed on by, and Nia finally reached her decision on rather or not she should move in with Black. Nia decided to follow her heart, and it was telling her to go ahead and move in with him. Nia knew that her mom wouldn't approve of her moving in with Black, so she didn't bother to ask her opinion. When Nia asked Charlene her opinion, Charlene told her that she was a grown woman and only she could make that decision. Asia told her that she thought they hadn't been dating long enough to be moving in together; Asia also told her that, whatever her decision she choose she would always be there for her as a friend.

Nia got all of her furniture out of her apartment and moved into Black's home. Black was so happy that they celebrated her first official day in his home over a nice quiet romantic dinner.

Nia waited two days before calling her mother to tell her the news. She knew that her mother wouldn't be thrilled to hear that she had moved in with her boyfriend.

Right before she dialed her mom's phone number, she took a deep breath and then picked up the phone and dialed the number. The phone rang three times before someone answered it. Just as Nia started to hang up, Mrs. Thompson answered the phone.

"Hello."

"Hi, Mom," said Nia.

"Oh, Nia. It's great to hear from you. I haven't heard from you in a while."

"Well, I'm doing fine, Mom."

"I tried to call you, but your phone number has been changed. You're not having a hard time paying your phone bill, are you?" asked Mrs. Thompson with deep concern.

"No, I'm not Mom. I just moved two days ago, and I called to give you my new phone number."

Nia had already told Charlene that she moved in with Black. From the way Mom was sounding on the phone, Nia knew that she didn't know. Nia was relieved that Charlene didn't tell her mother first, because she wanted to be the one to tell her the news.

"Mom, there's something I have to tell you."

"What is it, dear?"

"I moved in with Black," quickly replied Nia.

For a moment, there was nothing but silence. All Nia could hear was her mom's breathing.

"Mom, are you still there?"

"Yes, I'm still here, this just startled me a little."

"Well, what do you think?" asked Nia.

"What do you mean, what do I think! You should have asked me that before you did it!" angrily responded Mrs. Thompson.

"Mom, I was scared to mention this to you because I knew that you would react this way."

"What way is that, Nia? You mean upset! Well you're damn right I'm upset because you're making a big mistake! You saw what happened to Charlene!" yelled Mrs. Thompson.

"Mom, it's not going to happen to me, because Black loves and respects me. He's really a good man and has a lot going for himself. You'll see that when you come down here to visit."

"Let me calm down a second, Nia. All of this is hard to swallow at one time. You just hurt me, Nia. I don't want to see you get hurt or destroyed over some man. I love you so much, and I don't want to see your world come crashing down."

"Mom, I'm a grown woman, and I can take care of myself. I made it from being homeless on the streets, having a crackhead as a mother, and being abused by my step father. If I made it through all that, I can handle a simple heartbreak if it happens."

"Well, Nia, I really hope so. I hope that you're making the right decision."

"Mom, I feel like I am. I'll be all right."

"Well, this is your decision, so all I can do is deal with it and give you some moral support."

"Mom, when are you going to come and visit me?" asked Nia, trying to change that subject.

"I was thinking about coming sometime in May."

"Oh that will be great. I can't wait to see you, Mom."

"I can't wait, either."

"Well, Mom, I need to go now. It's about my bedtime."

"OK, Nia, but before you go, I just want you to know that, if you need me for anything at all, I'll always be here for you."

"Oh, thanks, Mom. I love you."

"And I love you, too, Nia."

The first two months of living with Black was wonderful; but after those two months, Nia began to see a side to Black that she hadn't seen before. She realized that Black was very dominating and possessive.

Sometime in January 1992, Nia noticed a change in Black's personality. Nia was about to go over to Asia's house so they could go to the mall. She was about to head out the door when Black blocked her path.

"And where do you think you're going?" he asked, Black gazing into her eyes.

"Black, I'm just going over to Asia's house. We're going shopping at the mall," answered Nia as she walked around him to head out the door.

Black grabbed Nia's arm and said, "Oh, no, you're not! You're going to stay home with me! Why do you always have to go out with that bitch all the time?"

"Black, you're being very unreasonable here. I've been in this house with you for the past two weeks, and today I've made plans to hang out with my girlfriend."

"But Nia, I need you here."

"Baby, I'll be back," said Nia as she tried to walk away.

Black grabbed Nia's arms again with an even firmer grip. "Black, what has gotten into you? Let go!" demanded Nia as she tried to break free of his grip.

Finally, Black let her go. Nia walked towards the door.

"Nia, if you walk out that door, you'll regret it!" said Black in a firm voice.

Slam! Nia walked out the door.

Who in the hell does that man think he is, thought Nia. He's trying to tell me what to do, he's not my damn father! And I'm sure as hell not going to let him start telling me what to do. What he had said really bothered her. Nia got in her car and drove off to Asia's house.

Meanwhile, Black reached inside the bar and took out some gin; he drank a couple of shots of it.

Secretly, Black had been drinking whenever Nia wasn't around. He had been very depressed lately, because he felt like things were falling apart.

Black's business was losing a lot of money because seventy percent of the companies he had contracts with were going through bankruptcies or mergers with larger corporations. Black had tried to get contracts with these large corporations but, they told him that they didn't want to deal with him because his business was too small. In reality, he knew the reason they didn't want to do business with him was because of the color of his skin.

He lifted another glass of gin and wept in sorrow. He was

angry that Nia was not there to make him feel better. All she wants to do is hang out with her girlfriend rather than me, he thought.

Then he thought that maybe she was fooling around behind his back. The intoxicating effect of the alcohol was causing his thoughts to become more irrational.

The thought of her messing around with another man made him furious. Black squeezed the glass in his hand so tightly that it shattered into pieces.

"Nia, you're going to regret this when you get back. You're not going to do that same little stunt on me again," whispered Black to himself.

Nia and Asia was at the mall having fun window shopping. Nia bought herself a new outfit and Asia bought a new pair of shoes. While looking in one of the store windows, Nia spotted the same shirt that Black had wanted two weeks ago. She bought the shirt for him and decided that she would surprise him with it. She thought that maybe a gift would cheer him up, especially since she knew that he has been very depressed lately.

After leaving the mall around 9:00, Asia and Nia decided to go to Taco Bell to eat. Then they went to Asia's house to talk. Nia was really concerned about the way Black has been acting lately, and she wanted to talk to Asia about it.

"Asia, Black has been acting very strange lately. He hasn't been acting like himself."

"It seems like he's going through something, Nia," suggested Asia. "You really think so?"

"Yeah, men are different from women. A lot of times it is harder for them to let out their emotions. As women, we would cry and open up by talking about our problems, but with men they tend to hold in their feelings."

"Asia, I believe you're right, maybe he's acting this way because he needs me to be there for him," agreed Nia.

"Maybe I shouldn't have left him alone, especially since he's having some problems with his business."

"Girl, you could have canceled going out with me. Your man is very important. I would have understood."

"Asia, thank you for your wonderful insight. I thought he was trying to be bossy, but maybe he was trying to reach out to me," said Nia.

"No problem, girlfriend, anytime."

"I'll see you later at work," said Nia as she walked out the door.

"OK, bye, Nia."

"Bye, Asia."

After leaving Asia's house at about 10:30, Nia headed back home. She unlocked the door and realized it was very dim inside.

"Black, I'm home."

"I see you," said Black in a deep rugged voice.

He clicked on the light.

"It's about time you decided to come back home," said Black with lack of emotion.

He walked towards Nia. Nia lay her purse and shopping bags on the couch.

"So, where have you been?" he asked as he stood in front of her.

Nia looked into his eyes and saw how blood shot they were. She smelled alcohol on his breath.

"I went shopping and ate dinner with Asia. Black, have you been drinking?" asked Nia with deep concern.

"Shut up! This is not about me, this is about you!" yelled Black as he pointed his finger in her face.

Nia was quiet for a moment and was quite shocked at how he had raised his voice at her.

"Didn't you hear me, I said where have you been?" roared Black as he grabbed her arms and shook her violently.

Tears sprung to Nia's eyes and slowly ran down her cheeks.

"Stop, Black! You're hurting me, please let go!" whimpered Nia as she winced in pain.

"Nia, I'm waiting for your answer!"

"Black, I told you that I was out with Asia." cried Nia.

Black reached up and slapped her violently across the face. He hit her with so much force that she landed on the floor.

Black grabbed Nia by her hair and forced her to stand up and then punched her real hard in the stomach. Nia landed on the floor again. She couldn't speak, she was hurting and too scared to say anything. She had told him the truth, but he didn't believe her.

"Girl, I know you're fuckin lying to me, and I'm going to call Asia myself to see if you was really there," roared Black.

Black left Nia crying on the floor. Nia slowly forced herself up. She walked to the bathroom and looked at herself in the mirror and saw that he had busted open her bottom lip, and blood was dripping down her chin. Nia wet a face towel to wipe off the blood.

Feeling a sudden strike of pain in her lower abdomen, Nia bent over and held her stomach. That night, she slept in the guess bedroom because she was too scared to sleep next to Black.

Nia couldn't believe that her dream was turning into a nightmare. She was starting to feel the same fear towards Black that she had felt towards her stepfather. The days were turning back to the way things were when she was a child suffering from abuse inflicted by her stepfather, except this time it was her own boyfriend. Nia balled up like a baby and cried herself to sleep.

Chapter #19

Black, called Asia to find out if Nia was telling him the truth. Asia told him that she had been with her last night. He began to feel guilty when he found out that Nia had been telling him the truth.

Later that afternoon, Black tried to patch things up with Nia. He casually walked into the guest bedroom and saw her sleeping on the bed.

"Nia, wake up," whispered Black, trying to wake her up.

Nia finally opened her eyes. She tried to get, up but winced from a sharp pain in her stomach.

Black reached over to push a strand of hair from her face, but she flinched and jumped back as he lifted up his hand.

Noticing her reaction, Black said, "Nia, I'm not going to hurt you. I just wanted to push your hair out of your face."

Nia was very quiet. She didn't have anything to say to him.

"Nia, I called Asia, and she told me that you was with her last night. I'm sorry.

"Sorry, is that all you can say after what you did to me last night? I didn't deserve that." uttered Nia.

"Baby, I didn't mean to hurt you. I got drunk, and my temper got way out of hand. I won't do this again," he added.

"Black, I don't know if I can trust you. You're my man, and

I'm suppose to feel safe around you. I'm not suppose to be scared around my own man," said Nia as tears filled her brown eyes.

"I know, and it won't happen again," said Black as he sat down next to her.

"I made your lunch," Black placed his strong arms around her.

"Thanks," said Nia as she looked down at the quilted comforter on the bed.

"You're trembling. Don't you believe me?" he asked.

"I don't know, Black," Nia responded honestly.

Black reached over and hugged her. She started to cry.

"Nia, I love you and I know I've hurt you, but please forgive me. I need you by my side. I'm going through so much turmoil in my life right now."

Nia hugged Black back and gave him another chance.

Meanwhile, Black continuously nagged Nia about getting on birth control pills. Black couldn't stand wearing condoms during sex. They both went to the STD clinic to get tested and they both tested negative for venereal diseases and AIDS. Since both of them didn't have AIDS and were not seeing other people, Black couldn't see why they had to use condoms.

Black pressured Nia so much that she asked her doctor to put her on the pill, just so she could get him off her case. Nia had become skeptical about Black after he hit her. Since Black hadn't hit her anymore, Nia was beginning to feel at ease with him and thought maybe she could trust him again.

After work, Nia went to her doctor. After she finished her menstrual cycle, she started her first pack of birth control pills.

While taking the pills, Nia became very sick; she felt very nauseous. Nia went back to the doctor to see if she could switch to

another type of birth control pills. Her doctor prescribed some new
pills, and she started taking them immediately. She felt much better
with the new oral contraceptive.

In May, Nia and Black had to move out of the house, because Black
could no longer afford the high mortgage payments. Fortunately,
Black had another house on the other side of town that he had been
renting out for several years. Nia was thankful they had somewhere
else to go.

Black began hitting Nia again. Right after they moved into
their new home, Nia begged Black to go to counseling for his drinking
problem, but he wouldn't listen to her. The more he drank, the worse
he became.

One day, Nia's mom came down to visit them for a week.
After a week, Mrs. Thompson had to go back to New York. Nia didn't
want her mom to go because she enjoyed her company and missed her
so much. She also didn't want her mother to leave because Black
didn't hit her while her mom was staying with them.

Mrs. Thompson didn't care for Black very much; she thought of
him as a selfish and dominating man. Mrs. Thompson told Nia several
times that she didn't like how he treated her and that she should leave
him.

Nia decided that she was going to take her mother's advice and
leave Black; she was sick and tired of him abusing her.

In June, Nia became very ill. She couldn't seem to keep food
in her stomach. Almost every time she ate something, she vomited.
She felt very tired and sluggish and even had migraine headaches.

At first, Nia thought she just had the flu, so she took cold
medicine and hoped she would feel better.

One day, Nia got very dizzy and passed out. Black came home and discovered her lying on the floor. He picked Nia up and took her to the bedroom and lay her on the bed. Black went to the bathroom and got a cool face towel with water and then returned to the bedroom to place it on her forehead.

When Nia finally woke up, she looked up and saw Black sitting on the bed next to her.

"Are you OK, Baby?" asked Black as he ran his fingers through her hair.

"Yeah, I'm fine. What happened?" asked Nia.

"I don't know, all I know is I found you laying passed out on the floor."

"Well, when I got home from work and took off my shoes, I blacked out. I can't remember anything after that," recalled Nia as she sat up and felt her temples throbbing.

"I think you better lay down and rest." Black noticed how sick she looked.

"Nia, you need to go to the doctor and get yourself checked out, because this isn't normal," stated Black with concern.

"Black, I'm fine," said Nia.

"No, you're not, Nia. You've been sick for over a month, and now I find you passed out on the floor."

"Well, I guess you're right. I'll set up an appointment tomorrow," said Nia.

"No, you're going to do it today. It is 4:30 and the doctor's office stays open till 5:30, so you have time to call."

Nia looked at Black and could tell he was dead serious. Nia was in no mood for arguing.

"OK, I'll call her up today," agreed Nia.

"Great, I'll get your doctor's phone number and pull the phone in the room for you," grinned Black.

"All right," mumbled Nia as she laid back down to rest.

The next day, Nia and Asia went out to lunch during their break.

"So, how have you been feeling lately? You're not still sick, are you?" asked Asia as she sat down at the table.

"Yeah, I still haven't been feeling my best lately, but I'm going to the doctor this Thursday to have a check up," responded Nia.

"What if?" questioned Asia as a thought just crossed her mind.

"What?" replied Nia.

"Oh, nothing. A silly thought just came to me," said Asia as she unwrapped her sandwich.

"What was you thinking about?" asked Nia as she took a bite into her sandwich.

"Nia, are you sure you're not pregnant, because all of the symptoms you mentioned to me makes it seem like you might be pregnant."

"Asia, I can't possibly be pregnant because I came on my period.

"Just because you came on your period doesn't necessarily mean that you're not pregnant because it happened to me when I was dating my ex-boyfriend, Todd."

"Yeah, I remember you telling me about Todd," recalled Nia.

"Well, when I got pregnant by Todd, about three and a half years ago, I was always sick, but I kept on having my periods. I went to the doctor to see what was wrong with me because I was tired of being sick all the time. And once I heard the news from the doctor that I was already four months pregnant, I got the biggest shock of my life."

"What ever happened between you and Todd," asked Nia,

munching on her fries.

"Oh, he left me when he found out I was pregnant," answered Asia while sipping her soda.

"Oh, my gosh, he was an ass hole! How could he leave you when you needed him the most?"

Nia couldn't understand how men could be such dogs, especially when they know they have a good woman right by their side.

"Well, that is the past, and I don't hold grudges. I just moved on with my life. I couldn't afford to raise a child on my own at the time, so I had an abortion," said Asia.

"If I was pregnant with Black's child, I would have an abortion too," mumbled Nia while finishing up her sandwich.

Nia was still hungry, she wanted to go back and buy another sandwich and a large order of fries. Lately she noticed that she had a very large appetite.

"What do you mean you would have an abortion? I thought you loved Black."

Asia was shocked to hear Nia say that. She knew that if she got pregnant by Kelvin, she would definitely want to have his child.

"Asia, it's just that we're having problems with our relationship. Ever since Black's business went down hill, he has been drinking heavily and hanging out with no good people. He even hits me whenever he gets angry, and lately I've been getting fed up with him."

"Dang Nia, I didn't know all of this was going on," said Asia as she swept her bangs from her eyes.

"Yeah, all of this has been going on. My mom doesn't like Black, she feels that he is very possessive and dominating over me."

"Now when I think about it Nia, he does mistreat you. I remember when I had to chew him out about disrespecting you in front of his friends a few weeks ago."

Asia recalled an incident that had happened about three weeks ago when Asia went to visit Nia at her new home; Black and some of his friends were watching football on T.V., and they ran out of beer.

Black yelled, "Nia, go get me and the fellas some beer from the refrigerator!"

Nia didn't hear Black; she was in the bedroom with Asia showing her some of the clothes that she had recently bought at the mall.

When Nia didn't get the beer for him and his friends, Black became enraged. He went into the bedroom and grabbed Nia's small arms. He cursed her out and he raised his hand as if he was about to slap her, but realized Asia was still in the room.

Asia saw that Nia was scared of him. As a good friend, Asia stood up for Nia and told Black off.

"Black, you have no right talking to her like that!" yelled Asia.

"Fuck you, Asia, this is between Nia and I. If you don't like it, your can take you black ass out of my house!" roared Black. After he told Asia off, Black finally released Nia's arms and left the room.

"I'm sorry, Asia. He's just in a bad mood. I better go in the kitchen and get the beer before he gets angrier."

"Nia, you don't have to put up with his bull shit," said Asia. Nia left the bedroom to get the beer.

Ever since then, Asia had not been over to Nia's house again.

Nia and Asia were both quiet as they thought about that afternoon.

Asia broke the silence. "Nia, why don't you take a home pregnancy test to see if you're pregnant?"

"Well I guess I could do that. I'll go to the drugstore right after work to pick one up. I don't want to take it at home, so do you

mind if I do it at your house? Because if I'm pregnant, I don't want
Black to know."

"Sure, no problem, Nia."

"Our relationship has been pretty fucked up lately. Being
pregnant will only make things worse," mumbled Nia.

After work, Nia and Asia went to the drugstore to buy a
pregnancy test. Once they got to Asia's house, Nia went straight to the
bathroom to take the test.

A few minutes later, Nia came out of the bathroom. She
walked into the kitchen and saw that Asia was washing dishes and
talking on the telephone.

Nia didn't want to disturb Asia, so she walked out of the
kitchen and went into the living room. Nia paced back and forth; she
kept on glancing down at her watch to see what time it was.

Finally, five minutes had passed. Nia went to the bathroom to
check on her test. Her heart started to beat very fast; she hoped that
it was negative.

She had read the directions and knew that plus means that
you're pregnant and minus means that you're not. Nia crossed her
fingers and looked down at the pregnancy test; she saw the plus sign.

Nia's heart sank when she saw that her test was positive.
she pulled the lid down on the toilet seat and then sat on it. She
sobbed for a moment and wiped her tears as she tried to get her mind
straight as to what she was going to do.

She decided that she was not going to tell Black at all. She
wanted to go to the doctor to see if the pregnancy test would still be
positive. Nia heard that in some cases home pregnancy tests were not
100% accurate and, in this case, she hoped that the test was wrong.

I don't want to be with a man who beats on me, and I sure as
hell don't want to bring a child up in the same type of environment I

lived in when I was growing up, she thought. The easiest thing for me to do is end my relationship with Black and have an abortion, thought Nia.

Before Nia left Asia's place, she told her the results. Asia was still on the phone long distance with one of her relatives that she hadn't heard from in a long time. Asia was about to get off the phone to talk to Nia about her situation, but Nia was not in the mood for talking. Nia left Asia's house and went home.

Thursday right after work, Nia went to the doctor's office. The doctor gave her a regular checkup and then gave her a pregnancy test. The doctor told Nia that she would call her back either Friday or Monday with the results.

Friday at work, Nia received a phone call from the doctor's office, but she was too busy to talk. The receptionist took a message for her.

Since the doctor's office couldn't reach Nia at her job, the nurse called her home phone number; Black was at home.

The phone rang two times before Black answered it.

"Hello?"

"Hi, may I speak to Nia Chevez?"

"Nia's not at home, may I take a message?"

"May I ask who I am speaking to?"

Damn, this person is awfully nosey thought Black.

"This is her boyfriend," he answered.

"Well, this is Dr. Strong's office, and I'm just calling Nia to give her results. Please tell her that her pregnancy test came back positive and tell her congratulations!" exclaimed the nurse.

"OK, I'll give her the message," said Black as he hung up the phone.

Dang, my baby is pregnant, he thought. The news brought a

smile to his face. At thirty going on thirty one, Black wanted to have a child. He thought that it was perfect timing. Even though he had lost all of his assets, he felt that God was blessing him with this child.

This means I definitely need to find me a job, thought Black. He picked up the newspaper and began looking under the job classifications.

No wonder she's sick all the time and eats like a pig, he thought. He had thought that she was pregnant, but she kept on reassuring him that she wasn't.

Black couldn't wait to tell her what he thought was very good news.

At 5:30, Nia finally got home from work. She was still not feeling very well; she had vomited several times at work, and she came home and vomited again. Nia couldn't understand why she was so sick, because when she was pregnant when she was sixteen, she didn't feel nearly as bad. Black heard Nia in the bathroom vomiting. He came into see if she was OK.

"Nia, are you all right?"

"Yeah, I'm fine," answered Nia, flushing the toilet and getting a damp face towel to wipe her face.

"All I need is some rest, and I'll be OK."

"Nia, before you lay down, I've got something to tell you."

"What is it, Black?"

"Your doctor called here and told me that you're pregnant."

"What?"

"Yeah, they said they tried to reach you at work, but you was busy, so they called here. I'm so happy," smiled Black.

Black continued talking, "I know that we are struggling right now because you're paying all the bills but I'm going to find me a job so that we will be able to take care of our child."

Nia was very upset that Black had found out about her pregnancy. It would make it more difficult for her to end their relationship and get an abortion. Black reached over and hugged Nia. He held her in his arms; he was so happy that she was having his child.

Nia was very surprised at his reaction. She had thought that he would be angry. Personally, she thought it was lousy timing for having a baby. She feared that having his baby would only make it harder for her to leave him.

Nia really loved Black with all her heart, but she couldn't tolerate his heavy drinking and violent temper. Lately she had found herself becoming quite fearful of him; she was afraid that he might lash out at her so violently one day that he might do her great harm. So many thoughts went through Nia's mind at once; she needed some time alone to figure out what she was going to do.

Chapter #20

Nia decided to have the baby. She went back to the doctor for her ultrasound and discovered that she was already three months pregnant.

Meanwhile, Black had found a job working as an electrician; he was disappointed that the only job he could find was part-time.

Nia and Black were still clashing in their relationship. Black sometimes felt that his manhood was being challenged by Nia, since she still made the most money. Often, Black felt that the only way he could show who was in charge was to putt Nia in check.

When Nia was six months pregnant, they got into a big argument, which turned into violence. The argument had begun over bills.

Nia felt that Black was being selfish; he didn't want to help pay the bills. Black thought that Nia was trying to challenge his authority.

"Nia, I just got paid this week, and I'm going to use it to try to build up my business again."

"But, Black, you have used all of your money on your business for the past two months, and I need you to help me pay some of these bills!"

"Come on Nia, I need for you to be more understanding right now because I'm trying to rebuild my business!"

"But, Black, I've been more than understanding. We're having a baby, and I need for you to help me pay some of our bills! Lately I've been coming out flat broke, because I've been paying for everything! You need to get your priorities straight!"

When Black heard Nia say that, it made him furious. He raised his hand up and violently hit Nia in the face. Black hit her so hard that she fell down and bumped her head against the wall.

"What you don't seem to understand is that I'm the man in this house, and what I say goes!"

Nia started crying. She was too scared to say anything else; she was afraid that he might hit her again.

Nia could taste blood in her mouth. She slowly sat up and gently rubbed the back of her head. Her head had banged against the wall so hard that she had a knot on the back of her head.

Black continued yelling at her.

"Girl, when are you going to learn that I'm the head nigga in charge! I guess I have to keep on beating your ass until you learn!"

Black started to take off his belt. Nia cried even harder because she knew exactly what he was going to do with it. Nia tried to move away from him.

"Black, please! I'm sorry, please don't!" she pleaded.

Black took off his thick belt and started to whip Nia all over her body with it. Then, he picked up an extension cord and whipped her with it also. Black whipped her so badly that it left marks and bruises all over her body.

"Fuck this bull shit, I'm leaving! Next time you'll know to shut the fuck up and keep your stupid ideas to yourself! Now you're going to pay the bills like I told you to and what I do with my money is my own fuckin business, not yours!" shouted Black.

After going off, he stormed out and slammed the door. Nia couldn't believe that he would beat her while she was expecting their child.

Nia couldn't understand what she did that was so wrong. She felt that she didn't deserve to be treated like this. She got up slowly; her skin was burning really badly. Nia looked at herself in the mirror and cried. She looked horrible.

Her nose was bleeding, and her lip was bleeding and swollen. Nia took off her clothes and rubbed her belly. She felt the baby move. She looked at her naked body in the mirror and saw and whip marks that cut deeply through her skin.

Nia went to the bathroom and took a shower to clean off some of the blood. Once the warm water hit her skin, it caused more pain. All Nia could do was wince and flinch. She felt the baby kick inside her womb. She looked down and gently rubbed her huge belly; Nia could tell the baby was upset. Whenever she became upset, the baby kicked harder as if, he too were feeling her hurt and pain.

Meanwhile, Black took off in Nia's Toyota Corolla. Black's Camaro had been repossessed, when he lost his business, and could no longer pay his car notes. And he had wrecked his BMW about a month ago; Black was drunk one night and ran his BMW into a ditch.

Ever since he lost his cars, he would hop into Nia's car most of the time without even asking.

Black drove very fast over to Shiela's house. Sheila was Black's other girlfriend. Sheila knew about Nia, but Nia didn't know about her.

Black had met Sheila at a bar about four months ago and he had been seeing her ever since. Although Black loved Nia, he sometimes wanted to be with someone else.

Right now, Black felt that Nia was very unattractive. Often Black picked at her and called her hurtful names like "fat pig", "fat bitch", and "rolly polly". His meanness lowered her self esteem.

Black reached Sheila's apartment complex. Shelia had two children and worked as a waitress at a bar. She was brown skinned with shoulder length hair, which was actually a weave.

Black knocked on the door and Shiela answered it.

"Hi, Baby, how are you doing?" asked Shiela. Black eyed her up and down and shook his head at how fine she was. Shiela had on a white see through night gown that revealed her well-built body.

"May I come in? Nia and I had an argument."

"Why, sure you can," replied Sheila in a sexy seductive voice. Black went in.

"Where are your kids?" he asked, looking around for them.

"Oh, they're spending the night with their grandmother," replied Shiela.

Shiela led Black to her bedroom. She sat on the bed and patted the bed, gesturing him to sit down next to her.

Shiela sat behind Black and started to massage his broad shoulders. She had rings on every finger; her hands were manicured with long tips and gold colored finger nail polish. Black had given her the money to get her weave and nails done. For the past few months, a lot of Black's money was being spent on Shiela.

"So, Sugar, what happened between you and Nia?" asked Shiela while still massaging his shoulder.

"Oh, she thinks I should start paying the bills since I have this new job, and she's being totally unreasonably selfish. She's making it seem like I don't help around the house when I do. She thinks that since she makes the most money she can start telling me what to do," said Black, trying to make Shiela feel sorry for him.

"Why, that no good heffa! Well Baby, you don't have to worry about that because I'll give you some loving." Shiela kissed his neck.

"I'm glad you're so understanding, Shiela."

Shiela stood before him and took off her white gown. She stood completely naked.

"Yeah, and here is some sweet pussy to make you feel better." Shiela leaned over and kissed his lips.

One thing lead to another, and then they had sex.

Black didn't care about Shiela much; he mainly thought of her as a golddigger and a whore. He knew that she slept with men to get something in return. But whenever he got upset, lonely, or horny, he went to her for a good fuck.

Meantime, Nia looked out the window and noticed that her car was gone.

"Damn it, why does he always have to run off with my car?" wondered Nia aloud. He already wrecked his car, and now he wants to wreck mines too, she thought.

Asia always asked Nia why he had to use her nice car and she always get stuck with his dirty old work truck. Asia despised Black with a passion, because of the way he continued to mistreat Nia. She felt that a jerk like Black did not deserve a good woman like Nia.

Nia was eight months pregnant with her child. The doctors could have told her what sex the baby was, but she wanted it to be a surprise.

The night of March 20, 1993, Nia started having some strong contractions. Black was out in the streets somewhere, so she couldn't get in contact with him.

Throughout Nia's pregnancy, Black had not been there for her.

Whenever she had a Lamaze class, he promised that he would be there but never showed up. Asia was the one who came with her to some of her Lamaze classes. Black also promised her that he was going to be there when she has the baby, but she didn't think that he was going to be there for her. Feeling abandonment made her heart ache, because he had broken every promise he had made.

Nia cried when she felt another strong contraction. These contractions felt different from the mild ones she had before. Nia knew that this baby was about to come.

Quickly she picked up the phone to call Asia.

"Hello?"

"Asia, it's me, Nia," frantically replied Nia.

"Girl, are you all right? You're not going into labor, are you?"

"Yes, I believe the baby is coming."

"How are you contractions? They're not close together, are they?"

"No, not yet, but they are very strong. Asia, please come over here. I need you with me. I'm so scared."

"OK, Nia, I'll be there as soon as possible."

Click, they both hung up the phone.

Asia rushed to Nia's house, getting there in fifteen minutes. Nia was already at the door with the things she would need in the hospital.

Asia helped Nia get in the car, and then she went around to the driver's side.

"Where's your car?" asked Asia.

"Oh, Black has it. I can't drive his truck, because it needs to be fixed."

Asia couldn't stand how Black was treating Nia; just thinking about it made her angry. She wished that Nia would come to her senses and leave him.

Asia just shook her head and backed out of the driveway; she knew that this was not the right time to tell Nia what she thought of Black.

The hospital was thirty minutes from Nia's house, but Asia got there in twenty minutes, due to her fast driving; she was thankful that she didn't get pulled over by the police.

Nia became more and more irritable as her contractions grew stronger. Once she was assigned to her room, Dr. Richard Smith came in to see if she had dilated enough to have the baby.

"Well Nia, how are you today? Your water has broke and it looks like this baby is about to come," stated the doctor with a smile.

"I'm fine. I'm just in pain, I believe a shot would help," replied Nia as she winced and started to sweat heavily.

"OK, I'll send an anastegiologist."

After writing something on Nia's medical chart, Dr. Richard Smith said, "Nia, I'll be back in a little bit to see how you're progressing."

Dr. Smith was a short, olive complexion, slenderly built man. He had dark brown hair with a bald spot in the middle of his head. He appeared to be in his late fifties because of the gray mixed in his hair. Dr. Smith also wore glasses and had a short stubby beard.

Moments later the Anastegiologist came in to give Nia a shot.

"Gosh Nia, I thought you said you was going to have this baby natural without any pain killers," said Asia.

"Well, that was before I felt this excruciating pain. Oh, Oh, Asia, these contractions are so painful! I want to hurry up and have this baby!" cried Nia.

Once the the shot was done, Nia began to feel alot better.

An hour has passed when Dr. Smith finally returned. He

checked to see if Nia had dilated enough.

"Nia, you still have a little ways to go. You have dialated eight centimeters. I see the shot is working," said the doctor.

"Yeah it is working and I feel much better. I can't feel my legs though." Nia ajusted her pillow.

"Don't worry it's only temporary. You'll get the feeling back in yours legs after the medicine wears off," added the doctor as he walked out.

A nurse came in to check Nia's IV and to check on the baby's heart rate.

Nia was still upset that Black was not there. Nia tried to clear her mind and think about peaceful things.

"Nia, I'm going to call Keith and tell him that I'm at the hospital," said Asia as she got up and headed towards the door.

"Asia can you do me a favor?"

"Sure what is it?"

"Could you also call around and try to find out where that mother fucker is because he promised me that he would be here when our baby is born!"

"OK."

Asia could tell that Nia was very pissed off with Black. Why won't she leave that no good nigga? wondered Asia. All he does is beat on her and disrespect her, she thought. Asia knew Nia could easily find herself another man, but Black had put her down so much that he had lowered her self esteem by making her believe that what he said about her was true.

After walking around the hospital looking for a pay phone, Asia finally spotted one on the second floor. Asia dialed Keith's work number and told him the news. He told her that he was coming after he locked up the restaurant.

Before hanging up with Keith, Asia asked him if he had seen Black because sometimes he ran into Black in the streets.

Keith hesitated for a moment before he spoke.

"Well, Asia, Black didn't want me to tell anyone this because he don't want Nia to find out."

"What do you mean? Is he keeping something from Nia?"

"Yeah," responded Keith.

"What doesn't he want anyone to know?" asked Asia in suspense.

"Asia, Black is messing around behind Nia's back. For the past few months, Black meets up with this waitress that works at a bar across the street from where I work," answered Keith.

"Do you think that he's still there?" asked Asia.

"Yeah, from the window I can see Nia's car parked in front of the building."

"Can you go over there and tell Black that Nia is having his baby and that she wants him here with her!" snapped Asia.

"Asia, are you upset?"

"You damn right I am! You should have told me this sooner! Black has no right treating Nia this badly because she is such a good person who is always willing to bend over backwards for anyone. She just don't deserve this kind of cruel treatment from anyone!"

"I know she is a good person, but Nia is going to have to break up with Black, not us. Are you going to tell Nia what I told you about Black?" asked Keith.

"You damn right I'm going to tell her because she needs to know what's going on!"

"Well, I'll go and tell Black the news when I lock up the restaurant," said Keith.

"All right. Thank you, Keith, and I love you."

"I love you, too. I'll be there as soon as possible."
"OK."

Asia walked back to Nia's room. When she reached Nia's hospital room, they were taking Nia to the birth room. Nia wanted Asia to be there with her while she had the baby.

After vigorously straining and pushing the baby out of her womb, Nia was exhausted.

"It's a boy!" exclaimed Dr. Smith, lifting the baby up so she could see him.

The baby appeared healthy and was covered in blood. Nia could hear her baby crying while they went to wash him up.

"Nia, it's a boy! Isn't that great?" exclaimed Asia. Nia nodded.

The nurse brought the baby over to Nia so she could hold him. He was so soft and cuddly in Nia's arms. Once he was placed in his mother's arms, he stopped crying as if he knew this was his mother and she was going to love and take good care of him. She counted each finger and toe to make sure they were all there. She kissed him gently on the forehead. Nia was so happy and tired at the same time.

After a while, the nurse took the baby, and Nia was taken to her room to rest.

Two hours later, Black and Keith reached the hospital. Asia spotted Keith and gave him a hug.

"Where's Nia?" asked Black.

He got some nerve acting like he's so concerned about Nia when he was out with another woman while she was having his child, thought Asia angrily.

"She's in the room sleeping. Where were you, Black? You know that Nia needed you tonight of all nights!" snapped Asia.

"Listen here, this is between Nia and I, so you need to stay out of our business!"

"Hold up, you two, we're here to see the baby, not fight," said Keith, breaking up an argument that was about to get heated.

Eventually, they got a chance to see the baby. Black smiled at his son though the glass window. The baby was light brown with a head full of pretty, soft, curly, black hair. Black smiled at him with pride. On the baby's name bracelet it read, "Carter."

The doctor told Black that the baby weighed five pounds and four ounces, and that he was a healthy baby. They also told him that Nia had named the baby Devonte Ramone Carter. Devonte Carter was born on March 21, 1993, at 12:00 midnight.

Later that night, Black sneaked into Nia's hospital room to see her. Even though it was after visiting hours, the nurse let him see her but told him that she was sleeping and should not be awakened until morning.

Nia looked so beautiful to him while in her sleep. He looked down at her long soft hair that cascaded down past her shoulders. He gently ran his fingers through her hair and gave her a kiss good night.

Chapter #21

After Nia came home from the hospital, Black continued to put her down about her weight. While she was pregnant with Devonte, she weighed 157 pounds. Right after she came back from the hospital, she weighed 142 pounds.

Nia knew that she was overweight and that most of her weight gain was due to her pregnancy; she was determined that she was going to lose the weight. Nia ignored Black's insults and started to exercise more. She joined an aerobics class at a local spa and also went power walking after she got off work.

Six months later, Nia had lost all of her weight. She was down to a size six and weighed 120 pounds. Nia looked at herself in the mirror and liked what she saw; she was proud of herself.

Not only did Nia see an improvement in her body, but Black saw it also. Many times, Black's friends came over to watch sports on T.V. and told him that he had a fine girlfriend. His friends couldn't understand why he was fooling around with Shiela when his girlfriend looked ten times better.

Black was getting tired of Shiela; every time he went over to visit her, she wanted money. Black finally dropped her because he knew that her didn't love her; the only thing he wanted from her was sex.

One Sunday afternoon, Nia decided to go over to Asia's house. Nia changed into some nice fitting Gap jeans and a light blue halter top. She took her hair loose from her pony tail and let her long thick mane flow down her back; Nia noticed that her hair had grown a lot. Gosh, I need to get my hair fixed, it's in great need of a touch up, she thought.

Devonte started crying, and Nia went to the crib to attend to him. She knew he was not hungry because she had just fed him. She checked his diaper, and sure enough, Devonte was crying because his diaper needed changing.

Nia reached inside her baby bag and took out a clean fresh diaper to change him. After she changed him, he stopped crying and smiled at his mother. Nia smiled at him and picked him up.

Devonte was a very sweet and good baby. The only time he cried was when he needed to be changed, or was hungry, or just wanted some special tender loving care. Nia held Devonte in her arms and kissed him gently on the cheeks.

"You're such a sweet baby...And Mama loves you so very much," said Nia in a high pitched voice.

At six months, Devonte was a chubby baby; he had a head full of hair and was a pretty chestnut complexion. Devonte was looking more and more like his father each day. Black couldn't possibly deny that Devonte was his son.

Nia dressed Devonte in a cute little outfit, a pair of blue shorts and a matching baseball shirt that Asia had given him.

"Guess what, Devonte? We're going over to your godmother's house to pay her a visit," said Nia, placing his whites socks on to his tiny feet.

In her heart, Nia felt that Devonte was the best thing that had happened in her life; she loved him with her entire heart. She felt that he was her gift from God. She couldn't imagine life without him. What she loved the most about little Devonte was that he loved her back in return.

Nia picked up Devonte and gently placed him in his carseat. Nia grabbed her things and picked Devonte up. When she went through the kitchen to pick up her keys, she saw Black in the den watching T.V.

Nia walked in the den and said, "Black, Devonte and I are going to Asia's house."

"OK," responded Black. He had a Bud Light in one hand and the remote control in the other.

Black's eyes were glued to the television screen.

Nia went outside and locked the door behind herself. She walked to her car and unlocked the passenger side. Then she put Devonte in the back seat, placed the seatbelt securely across him and the carseat, and got in herself

Every time Nia went any where, she had to tell Black where she was going or else he would go into his crazy violent mood swing. But every time he went out somewhere, he wouldn't tell her where he was going, and she knew not to dare ask him.

Often Nia was scared to walk into her own house. She knew that she shouldn't feel that way, but she always felt unsafe. Black was so unpredictable that she didn't ever know when his temper would get out of hand.

Nia tried to please Black in every way possible in order to avoid a beating. She would always try to have dinner fixed on time and would always bring him his beer while sports were on T.V.

Nia thought about the conversation that she had overheard among Black and his friends. They were talking about women and relationships, and from their conversation, they all sounded like power hungry men who loved dominance and had serious ego problems.

Nia remembered hearing Black say, "A woman is like a child, you have to train her to obey her man...many times it just takes a good old fashion ass whipping for her to learn..."

Finally, Nia arrived at Asia's house. Asia's car was parked in the parking lot, so she figured Asia was probably home.

Nia rung the doorbell, and Asia answered it.

"Hi, girl! Oh, you brought the baby with you! Oh, let me hold him! He's so precious!" exclaimed Asia as she reached over to hold him.

Nia handed Devonte to Asia, and she held him in her arms. Nia walked in behind Asia and locked the door.

"So, how are things going for you?" asked Nia.

"Oh, I'm doing just fine. You know I'm still trying to get my own business started so I don't have to keep on working at the dentist office for the rest of my life. I want to do something new; I want to better myself."

"You know what, Nia?"

"What?" questioned Nia.

"You need to start thinking about bettering yourself, too," replied Asia, still snuggling Devonte closely.

"You know what? You're right. I do need to start thinking more about my future, especially now that I have someone else to think about other than myself," agreed Nia with a smiling nod at Devonte.

"You can do better just by leaving that no good boyfriend of yours," suggested Asia as she sat down on the sofa and put Devonte on her lap.

"Come on now, Asia," mumbled Nia. She didn't want her talking badly about Black.

"Nia, there's something I been meaning to tell you."

"What is it?" asked Nia.

"Well I should have told you sooner, but Keith thought I should just stay out of your business, but I believe you should know the truth about Black."

Devonte started crying, so Asia handed him back to Nia. Nia held Devonte in her arms while she got his pacifier from her bag. She placed the pacifier in his mouth and he stopped crying.

"What is it, Asia? It sounds very serious."

"Nia, while you was pregnant, Black was fooling around behind your back with this woman name Shiela. I don't know if he's still seeing her now but I know that he was seeing her while you was expecting. Keith told me that Black would drive your car to the bar across the street from his job to meet up with her when she get off work as a waitress. Sometimes Keith saw Black driving her in your car! The reason why he never had money to help you pay the bills was because he was spending it on her."

"Asia, are you sure this is really true? Because if it is, it really answers a lot of questions I was wondering about."

"I swear I am telling you the truth, Nia. I wouldn't lie to you because you are my most dearest friend in the whole wide world."

"So, this explains why a woman name Shiela used to call Black all the time. She would leave messages on the answer machine asking for him to call her back. All of this makes so much sense to me now. So that's why he always had to run off with my car at night! Oh, my gosh, how could I have been such a fool!" cried Nia, seeing the awful truth for the first time.

"Girl, it's going to be all right. Everyone has been played on before, and it's not the end of the world. It may hurt right now, but things will get better for you, you'll see," Asia sat next to Nia and gave her a hug.

"Come on, let's go to the mall and go shopping. I'll take you out to dinner, maybe that will make you feel better."

An hour later, they left and went to the mall.

Two weeks passed, and Nia was still with Black, even though she had found out that he had been messing around behind her back. The only reason she stayed with him was because she wanted Devonte to have a father, even though Black was not a good one. Most of the time when Devonte cried and needed some attention, Black would not even lift a finger to help.

On Friday, Nia had to work late at the dentist office, so she called Black and asked him if he would pick Devonte up from the nursery. Black told her that he wasn't going to pick him up, because he planned on going out with his friends.

Asia saw that Nia was upset after getting off the phone with Black. Since Black refused to help out, Asia picked Devonte up, and he stayed at her house until Nia came over to pick him up after she got off from work.

Nia was really opening up her eyes and starting to see the bad side of Black. She noticed that Black could be the most selfish man in the whole world.

Black was even selfish when it came to sex. He always came before Nia had a chance. Instead of enjoying foreplay together, he forced himself inside of her. Sometimes she felt that he got a kick out of seeing the painful look on her face while they were making love.

Lately, Nia hated having sex with Black; she felt that he was too rough. Sometimes she would bleed afterwards and feel very sore. Instead of feeling pleasure, she felt pain during intercourse. She feared him so much that she slept with him to avoid his brutal beatings.

Later the same night that Black had refused to pick up

Devonte, Nia looked out the window and noticed that it was raining hard. She looked down at her watch and saw that it was already midnight. Nia was glad it was Friday, so she decided that she was going to stay up late and watch some t.v. in the den.

Nia flipped through the channels until she found a movie that caught her attention. The movie she watched was an old love story with Harry Belafonte and Dorothy Dandridge starring in it; the name of the movie was Carmen.

An hour later, Nia dozed off to sleep with the T.V. still on. She was suddenly awakened when she heard a loud knock on the door.

When Nia unlocked the door, Black stumbled in. He looked pitiful; his clothes were soaked from being out in the rain. The way he stumbled into the house indicated that he was drunk. He was so drunk that he was unable to unlock the front door.

Nia hated it when Black got drunk, because he could be very violent. Nia helped him up the stairs and out of his wet clothes.

While Nia tried to help him take off his wet jacket, Black kept on fondling her breasts. At first Nia didn't react, but Black was starting to annoy her because she was in no mood to have sex. Nia was angry with him for coming home intoxicated.

Black kept on grabbing and feeling on her breasts, so she started to move his hands off of her. Nia put Black's strong arm around her shoulder while she tried to help him up the stairs. Black was very heavy; he weighed about 215 pounds.

"Baby, how about some pussy tonight?" laughed Black as he smacked and grabbed her butt real hard.

"Ouch, that hurts Black, don't do that!" snapped Nia, rubbing her butt.

Finally, they reached the bedroom.

"Now, Black, let me help you out of your clothes so you can

lay down."

Nia unbuttoned and took off his shirt and then she helped him out of his wet pants and socks.

"Now you can lay down and rest."

When Nia tried to help him lie down on the bed, Black pulled her down with him; Nia was lying on top of him.

"Black, what are you doing? Let go!" ordered Nia.

Black rolled over on the bed so that he was on top and she was on the bottom. Black started to kiss her roughly on the lips and grabbed her breasts underneath her shirt.

"No, Black, stop it!" yelled Nia.

Black slapped her brutally across the face.

"Shut the fuck up, bitch!" he sneered.

Nia could smell the alcohol on his breath.

In the other room, Devonte started crying. Nia tried to get up to get her baby, but Black shoved her back down.

"Black, please let go! I need to check on Devonte!" pleaded Nia.

"What did I tell you, I told you to shut the fuck up!" yelled Black. He hit her some more, inflicting so much pain that she became trapped by her fear.

"Now, you forget the baby because you're going to satisfy me tonight!" demanded Black.

Black pulled up her skirt and pulled down her panties. He ripped open her blouse and started roughly sucking on her nipples. Nia started crying, she couldn't stop him. He held her hands down with one of his huge hands.

Nia tried to push him off, but he was too strong and heavy. Black forced himself inside her. She kept on crying with pain; he was hurting her.

Nia couldn't believe that this was happening to her.

"Black, please stop, you're hurting me!"

"Good!" sneered Black as he continued to rape her.

Finally Black let her go. Nia ran to Devonte's room and locked the door. She held her baby in her arms. All she could do was cry. Nia knew in her heart that it was definitely time to leave this man. She knew that she could no longer put up with his abuse. She made up in her mind that she was going to take Devonte and move out as soon as she could manage it.

About a month later, Devonte was showing signs of teething. He became very irritable because his gums were very sore.

On a Friday night, Black's friend Edward came by the house to watch boxing on HBO. Black left to buy some more beer and Edward stayed behind.

After Black left, Edward left the den and walked into Nia's bedroom. Nia was folding clothes and her back was towards him. Nia turned around because she felt like someone was watching her; she discovered Edward standing in the door watching her.

"Hi, Edward, you almost gave me a heart attack. I thought you left with Black to get some beer," said Nia as she turned back around and continued to fold more clothes.

"Oh, I decided to stay behind." Edward walked on in.

Edward was about five feet, eight inches tall and had a light skin complexion. He was medium build and had a mustache and goatee.

"There's a question I've been wanting to ask you," said Edward.

"What is it you wanted to ask me?"

"I want to know why such a beautiful woman like yourself is

doing with a loser like Black. He treats you with no respect."

Nia couldn't believe that Edward was talking about Black like that; she thought that they were friends.

"I thought you and Black were friends, you shouldn't talk about him like that," said Nia.

Edward came closer and lightly touched her pretty hair. Nia pushed his hand away from her.

"Why be with him when you can be with me?" said Edward with a mischievous grin.

Quickly, Nia moved away from him. Edward continued to approach her.

"Get away from me, Edward!"

Edward stood right in front of her again.

"You may love Black, but does he really love you?" He looked down at her and gently held her chin. Nia looked up at him and he gazed down at her. He leaned over like he was about to kiss her, but Nia turned her head away from him.

"Edward, get away from me because I see now that you are a backstabber! You're not Black's friend!"

"I'm his friend, all right, but when the brother is wrong he's wrong. He has a good thang and he doesn't even realize that it's you. I'll leave you alone, but I'll tell you one thing, if you was with me, I wouldn't be treating you this badly, I would treat you right. One day you'll come to your senses," said Edward with a grin.

He walked out of the bedroom. Before he left, he winked at her and eyed her up and down and said, "I definitely want to have a piece of that."

Nia was glad he had finally left her alone. She couldn't stand Edward; he always thought that he was a lady's man. He was definitely the pretty boy type, light skin with curly hair cut into a short fade. He reminded Nia of the singer Christopher Williams who played in the movie, *New Jack City*.

Edward had always came on to Nia. Every time he saw her, he always gave her compliments. Whenever Black was not looking, he would smile and try to make eye contact with his piercing eyes. He even called their house several times to try to talk to her and not Black. Nia didn't trust Edward; she thought of him as sneaky and deceitful, that's why she always kept her distance from him.

The next day, which was Saturday, Black was furious with Nia; he came home that evening in a rage. Edward had lied to Black and told him that something had happened between him and Nia; he told Black that he had sex with Nia. Black lost his temper to the point that he couldn't think clearly.

After driving home like a mad man, Black unlocked the front door and then slammed it shut behind him.

"Nia, come here, now!" he ordered. Nia heard Black and could tell that he was angry about something; she just hoped that he wasn't upset with her.

"Yes, Black," Nia walked into the room.

Nia could have sworn that she saw fire in his eyes. She was scared.

"What's going on between you and Edward?" demanded Black.

"Nothing is going on between me and Edward," answered Nia honestly.

Nia watched Black ball up his huge hand and punch the kitchen counter with a loud thump. He knocked all the dishes sitting on the counter down on the floor. Some of the plates and glasses shattered on the floor.

"Black, Edward came on to me, but nothing happened," said Nia as she moved away from him.

All the commotion woke Devonte from his sleep, and he began to cry. Black grabbed Nia's small arms and shook her violently.

"Now, I'm going to beat your ass for lying to me!" he yelled.

Black was getting tired of hearing the baby's wailng cry.

"I'm going to shut Devonte up. Maybe I'll have to teach him a lesson, too!" roared Black.

"Black, don't you dare touch him! He's only a baby!" yelled Nia,trying to break his iron grip.

"Who are you talking to like that?"

He smacked her across the face. Black had so much rage in him that he beat Nia until she laid unconscious on the floor. Black tried to revive her like he usually did, but this time it didn't work. He noticed that she was bleeding heavily from her nose and her mouth. He also noticed a big cut on her forehead from where he had rammed her head violently against the wall two times.

"Nia, please wake up! Please! I'm sorry, I didn't mean to hurt you!" pleaded Black as he held her in his arms.

He cried as he dialed 911 for the ambulance. Black prayed and begged God to not let Nia die, because he really loved her. He promised himself that he would stop drinking and stop hurting Nia and his son.

The police and the ambulance finally arrived. All the neighbors were outside watching and trying to see what was going on. The ambulance took Nia to the hospital. The police officers took Devonte and arrested Black for battery, because he admitted beating Nia. One of the police officers placed handcuffs on him while the other one read him his rights.

Chapter #22

Nia was rushed to the hospital, where the doctors discovered that she was suffering internal bleeding and a severe concussion. She was taken to surgery.

Meanwhile, Black was in jail. Black called Asia and asked if she would pick up Devonte from the jail. Asia asked him a lot of questions about what was going on, but he hung up; he didn't feel like going into details with Asia.

Once Asia got to the police station, she approached the officer working the front desk.

"Hi, I'm here to pick up the Devonte Carter."

"Are you Asia Roberts?"

"Yes, I am."

"OK. Derek Carter told us that he wants you to keep his child for him while he's in jail."

"What he's in jail for?" asked Asia.

"Battery. He beat up his girlfriend so badly that she had to be rushed to the hospital."

"Oh, my gosh! Do you know which hospital she's at?" asked Asia as she held her hand over her mouth in disbelief.

"She's at Lincoln Memorial Hospital. Officer Jones has Devonte, she's about to bring him to you. He's a cute little fellow." A smile came across the officer's face.

Later, Officer Jones came out with Devonte. Devonte appeared very calm; he had his pacifier in his mouth. Once the police officer approached Asia, Devonte leaned towards Asia with his short chubby arms and smiled; he knew exactly who Asia was. Asia got Devonte and held him in her arms. He kept on grabbing her large dangling earrings, so she had to take them off before he yanked them off.

"Do you know if it's possible for me to see Black?" asked Asia.

"Well, he said that he doesn't want to be bothered with anyone," answered the desk officer.

"Well, OK. Thanks for everything. Bye."

"You're welcome, good bye."

He's lucky he didn't want to see anyone, because if I saw him, I would curse him out, thought Asia. Asia was very worried about Nia, so she took Devonte with her and drove to the hospital to find out about her condition.

Thirty minutes later, Asia arrived at the hospital. With Devonte in her arms, she went inside to the information desk and asked about Nia.

"Nia Chevez is in surgery. Upstairs, on the fourth floor."

"OK, thanks."

Asia got on the elevator and went to the fourth floor. She went to the nurses' station to ask about Nia. A nurse told her that Nia was beaten very badly and was suffering from a severe concussion. The nurse also told her that she also had a fractured jaw, a punctured kidney, two broken ribs and that she was still in surgery.

Asia sat down in the waiting room with Devonte in her lap. Several hours passed before the doctor finished surgery on

Nia.

Dr. Linda Grant, Nia's doctor, approached Asia.

"Hi. The nurse told me you're here for Nia."

"Yes, I'm a close friend of hers."

"Well, Nia was injured pretty badly, but she's going to be OK. She's in recovery, she's going to do just fine."

After staying three weeks in the hospital, Nia was released. Asia kept Devonte while Nia was in the hospital. Nia stayed with Asia until she got well.

About a month had passed, and Nia was still unable to return to work; the doctors told her that she needed more time to heal. Black was still in jail and almost every single day, he called Nia.

Asia hoped that Nia would stay with her until she got herself together. She prayed that Nia wouldn't drop the criminal charges on Black or go back to him once he got out of jail.

Six months after the beating, Nia was finally well enough to go back to work. Dr. Grant recommended Nia go to group counseling for battered women.

Nia went to some of the group sessions. Asia was so proud that she was going to get some help. Nia's life appeared to be changing for the better. It seemed as if she was heading in the right direction.

In April 1994, months after the beating, Nia got a phone call from Black; begging for her to come visit him in jail. Two days later, Nia went down to visit Black. The guard walked Nia into a room. Nia entered the room and sat down in a chair that was across from a glass window.

Through the window, Nia saw Black walking into the other

room. He had on a gray-colored prison uniform. Black was much thinner, and he looked like he hadn't shaved in days. His hair was not neatly cut.

The guard took off Black's handcuffs, and he sat down across from Nia. Black picked up his phone first and gestured for her to pick up.

Nia picked up the phone and said, "Hi."

"Hello, Nia, how are things going for you?"

"Oh, fine."

"How's Devonte?" asked Black.

"Devonte is doing fine," answered Nia, glancing down at her hands.

"You're as beautiful as ever," whispered Black, staring at her through the glass.

"Thank you," Nia said shyly as she looked at him.

"Nia, I'm sorry about what happened. You know I love you, and I want us to get back together when I get out."

"Well Black, I don't think that's a good idea, because your temper has not improved, instead it's gotten worse."

"But, Nia, I love you. I need you and Devonte in my life. I promise that this time things will change." Tears started to form in Black's eyes.

Oh Lord, not this again, thought Nia. Nia knew he was going to start crying; he always did that to try to make her feel that what he was saying was really sincere.

"Black, don't start that teary eyed bull shit with me, because I'm sick and tired of you beating on me, being unfaithful, not helping to pay the bills, and not spending time with our son!"

"Nia, you have a lot of good reasons to be angry with me. The only thing I can do is admit that I was wrong, especially for that night

I hurt you so badly that you had to be rushed to the hospital," Tears rolled down his cheeks.

"I was devastated when I found out that you was telling me the truth about Edward. I should have had more trust in you," uttered Black, wiping tears with his white handkerchief.

"How did you find out that I was telling you the truth?" asked Nia curiously.

"Edward told me when he came by to visit me about a month ago. He told me that he was just playing a joke on me and that he didn't think that I would go as far as to beat you up," answered Black.

"Black, you still didn't tell me why you begged for me to come over to see you."

"Well, Nia, I'm getting out on parole for good behavior in the next couple of months. I wanted you to come here to visit me because I wanted to tell you that I love you and I wanted to see you again. I want us to be together as a family."

What Black told Nia really touched her deeply; she always wanted a family of her own. Maybe I should take him back, thought Nia.

"Will you please give me another chance? I'm begging you because I need you in my life, Nia. Without you and Devonte, I have nothing," cried Black.

Black's tears had made her teary eyed, too. Once again, she had fallen for Black's tears. once again.

"Black, I'll give you another chance. I love you, and I want us to start over from scratch."

Black lifted his hand to the glass, and Nia lifted her hand to his. The guard told him that his time was up, and it was time to go.

"Well, Nia, I have to go. I love you."

"I love you too, Black. I'll be here on the first of June."

When Nia told Asia the news, Asia was upset. She couldn't believe what she was hearing.

"But Nia, why are you going back to that no good nigga? He almost killed you the last time!"

"Asia, I love him and he said he loves me, too. He promised me he won't do it again.

"What about Devonte and your group counseling?"

"Well, Devonte is going to do just fine, because he has a mother and a father who love him very much. I don't feel that I have to go to counseling anymore because I feel fine.

"But Nia-!"

"Asia, come on now, I don't want to argue about this, because I've already made up my mind!" rudely interrupted Nia.

"Well, if that's how you feel. But if he hits you again, Nia, you know you'll always have a place to go to," said Asia.

"Thanks, but I don't think he will, because I really do believe he has changed," replied Nia as she hugged Asia.

Asia looked at Nia and knew that what she was doing was stupid and wrong; she did not believed that Black had changed in such a short period of time. She hoped that he didn't end up killing Nia. Asia couldn't understand why Nia was so desperate to try to receive love from a man who didn't show it or give it to her.

Nia always gave all her love to Black, but all he did was take it and stomp all over it, thought Asia.

"Nia, I still don't agree with what you are doing, but I really hope you will continue going to your therapy."

"OK, Asia, I'll do that if it will make you happy, because I know that you're going to stay on me until I do go back to counseling."

"You damn right I am," agreed Asia.

Asia looked at Nia and saw that she was rubbing her temples and had a painful look on her face.

"Nia, are you OK?"

"I've been having migraine headaches and dizzy spells since Black beat me up, but I'll be fine. It will go away after a while," replied Nia.

Asia thought that Nia looked much better than she did just after the battering. Now, she had a large scar on her forehead and it was the only outward reminder of her ordeal. When Asia fixed Nia's hair, she put a long bang in front to cover the scars on her fore head.

Nia's ribs and kidney were healed, so she didn't have to wear a bandage around her abdomen anymore. And her jaw was fine now. When she first came out of the hospital, Nia had to eat liquid food since she couldn't chew food with her jaw. Now, Nia was thankful that she could eat solid food again.

On June 1, 1994, Black was released from jail. Nia was so happy that he was finally out. The first week Black was out of jail, Nia saw improvement in the way he was acting. He was not drinking, and he seemed to have his temper under control. Nia was so glad that Black was finally spending a little bit of time with his son, who was now one years old.

But on the second week after his release from jail, Black started back into his old ways. He was hanging out with Edward, and he also started back drinking.

Eventually, Black broke his promise to Nia when his temper got out of hand. He kicked Nia in the stomach and smacked her violently across the room. That was the last time Black beat Nia, finally, she had enough.

Once Black left the house, Nia packed up all of her and

Devonte's belongings. She got Devonte and they left in her car. Nia didn't look back over her shoulder; this was the complete end to their relationship. Nia never went back to Black again.

Chapter#23

For two months, Nia stayed with Asia until she saved up enough money to move into her own apartment. In September, Nia finally had herself situated in her own two bedroom apartment.

Nia had not spoken to Black in over a month. She didn't want to be bothered with him. Asia told Nia that Black was still calling and asking to speak to her. He still didn't know that Nia no longer lived with Asia. Nia didn't want Black to know that she was living on her own. In some ways, she still feared Black; she didn't know what he would do to her if he saw her and had her alone.

Nia still loved Black, but she knew that he wasn't going to change. She knew that she couldn't possibly make him change, because only he could do that for himself.

In October, 1994, Black found out that Nia was not living with Asia. He followed her from her job to her new apartment. Black also got Nia's new phone number and started calling her every day. Often, he called her house and then hung up once she answered the phone. There were times when he threatened her over the phone and left obscene messages on her answer machine. Nia had to get her phone number changed several times, and the horrible phone calls eventually came to an end.

For the past few months, Nia continued to go to a battered women's shelter for counseling. Going to the group therapy sessions inspired and encouraged her to move on with her life. Black begged Nia to see him but she refused to have anything to do with him.

In November, Black finally joined in Alcohol Anonymous to get help for his drinking problem. It took Nia's leaving him for him to admit he had a problem.

Nia didn't want her son to grow up seeing his father beating his mother; she didn't want Devonte going through the same things she went through when she was a child. Nia wanted the best for her son; she wanted to raise him in a peaceful and loving environment, in which he would grow up to be a strong black man.

Since Nia had started on her new path to a better life, she was finally doing some of the things she had always wanted to do. The first thing Nia did do was to start going back to church and building up her faith in God. And the second thing she wanted to do was go back to school and better herself.

Nia realized that what Asia had been telling her was right, that she should start looking out for herself and thinking more about her future. Nia knew she didn't want to be a dental hygienist for the rest of her life she wanted more out of life, so she decided that going to college was an excellent start to bettering herself.

Leaving Black was the best decision that Nia had ever made. For the first time in a long time, she felt free. When she came home from work, she was no longer afraid. She didn't have to shoulder the burden of feeling like a nobody, because Black was not there to put her down and lower her self-esteem. Since Nia had left Black, she felt better about herself and her self-esteem was on the rise.

Even though Nia found out that Black was faithfully attending

Alcohol Anonymous meetings and had gotten his business off the ground, Nia still didn't go back to him. She made up her mind that she didn't want to be with Black anymore, regardless of how much he had changed his life.

Nia continued to let Black see Devonte because she felt that a father should be an important part of his son's life.

Many times, Black came on to Nia when he came over to visit Devonte. Every time he saw Nia, he would ask her out, but she always managed to turn down every single one of his offers.

One time when Black came over to visit Devonte, Black became very aggressive and was determined that he was going to have his way with Nia. Once Black put Devonte to bed and he drifted asleep he went into the kitchen to be with Nia.

Nia looked good to him. She had on a pair of snug-fitting black jeans and a white summer top that revealed the fullness of her breasts. Black watched from the doorway as she washed dishes. Nia had her hair pulled up into a ponytail with a few tendrils of hair still resting on her shoulders. Black found that very sexy.

He came up behind Nia and placed his arms around her small waist.

"Black, what are you doing?"

"I'm giving my baby a hug."

Nia turned around and looked up at him.

She took his hands off her waist and said, "Black, I'm no longer your baby. I told you that we're only friends."

"Come on, Nia, lets' do it one time for old time's sake," suggested Black, gazing into her eyes. Nia suddenly began to feel very uncomfortable.

"Black, I think that you should leave."

Black leaned over and started to kiss Nia firmly and roughly on the lips. Nia's hand quickly flew to push him away. Black pulled Nia closer to him and forced her to kiss him. His hands casually moved down to her butt and then up to her breasts; he gently caressed and squeezed her breasts. Nia turned her head away from him, and tears filled her eyes.

"Black, stop it! I said no and I mean it, so let go!" yelled Nia.

Black ignored her and continued to grope her. Nia tried to break free of his iron grip, but he was too overpowering. She starting crying; she was afraid that he was going to rape her again.

Black finally released her. Once he let her go, Nia reached up and slapped him as hard as she could. She picked up a knife.

"Don't you ever do that to me again motherfucker, or I swear I will kill you!" screamed Nia at the top of her lungs. She tried to stab him but she missed.

"OK, fine! If it's going to be that way, I'll leave," Black left quickly.

Black never tried to take advantage of Nia again. He knew that she meant what she said about killing him.

It had been five months since Nia left Black, and now she felt more stable than she did when she was with him.

Now when Nia saw herself in the mirror, she saw a different person. She saw a woman who possessed both inner and outer strength, a strength which had come when she accepted God back into her life; God had shown her the light and Nia saw that she had a spiritual glow.

Chapter #24

Nia looked out her window and enjoyed the beautiful scenery of San Diego; she was intrigued by the lovely weather. Even though it was almost winter, the temperature hovered at seventy-eight degrees.

It was the month of November and the year 1994, when Asia called Nia with her great news.

"Hi girl. It's me, Asia!"

"How are you doing? What's going on? You sound like you just won the lottery!" exclaimed Nia.

"Girl, I'm so happy, because something special happened to me last night!" beamed Asia on the other line.

"What happened?"

"Nia, Keith proposed to me last night!"

"No, girl! For real? Oh, I'm so happy for you!"

"He just got on his knees and in the restaurant asked me if I would marry him, and I said yes!" giggled Asia.

"Girl, that's wonderful! You and Keith make such a cute couple and you two have been together for a long time, almost three years. I was wondering when he was going to pop the question."

After talking to each other for a while about the future wedding and honeymoon, Nia and Asia got off the phone. Nia was so happy for Asia; she knew that she deserved a good man like Keith.

Asia had told Nia about the terrible experiences she had with men in the past; at one time, Asia believed there was no such thing as a good man, but her belief changed when she met Keith.

God blessed Asia with a good man and that proved to Nia that there was really a such thing as a good black man. Asia told her countless times that she, too, could find a good man. She felt that Nia should move on with her life.

That night, Nia called her mother to tell her she was doing fine. Since she hadn't spoken to her in a while. Nia didn't want her mother to start worrying about her.

When Nia told Mrs. Thompson that she left Black, Mrs. Thompson was so happy; she had never liked Black.

"Now, Nia, I'm so glad you left him. When I first saw him, for some reason I despised him. It seemed to me that he was like the devil trying to walk into your life and ruin it."

"Mom, Devonte is about to turn two years old in March. He still hasn't seen his grandmother in person, so the two of us are flying to New York to pay you all a visit."

"Oh really, Nia? That will be wonderful!" exclaimed Mrs. Thompson. "So when are you all coming?" asked mama.

"Oh, we're going to fly over there in February, because I'll be able to take two weeks off from work. I want to spend some time with my family. I miss you all so much."

"And we miss you, too, Nia," said Mrs. Thompson.

"How's Charlene doing?"

"Great!"

"Did she receive the her graduation gift I sent her?"

"Yes, and she told me to tell you thank you," answered Mrs. Thompson.

"Did I tell you that Charlene is dating someone new?"

"No, Mom, who is he?"

"Well, she's dating this Jamaican guy name Carl."

"Oh, really, that's fantastic! Do you like him, Mom?"

"I like him a lot. I feel that this might be the right man for Charlene. He's very good to her. He respects her and seems to be a nice young man..."

Once Nia got off the phone with her mother that night, she bathed Devonte and got him ready for bed. She read him a story, and later he drifted off to sleep. Nia closed the book and kissed him good night on the forehead.

Nia walked out of Devonte's room and headed for the kitchen. It was 8:00, time for her to hit the books and study for her exam. She was enrolled at San Diego University as a freshman; she had decided to major in psychology. Nia admired the psychologist who had counseled her at the battered women's shelter. She felt that counseling was something she would like to do in the future.

The most important person in her life was her son and she didn't have time to focus on anyone else. She liked being single because she is finally getting a chance to discover herself and doing some of things she always dreamed of doing, such as going to college and raising her son.

What Nia liked most about living on her own was having her independence. She liked being her own person and not having to change herself into something that she was not, just to satisfy and please another person.

As time progressed, Nia no longer feared Black; she could stand up to him now. Whenever he came over to visit Devonte, he tried to tell her what to do or come on to her sexually. Nia got so tired of Black always trying to dominate her and take advantage of her that she started putting him in his place or by simply kicking him out of her apartment. Nia knew that he no longer ruled her life.

After Black, Nia didn't date anyone for a while; it had been about eight months since she had been out on a date. Nia made a promise to herself that no man was ever going to hurt her again; she built a solid wall around her heart to keep any man from breaking her heart into a million pieces.

Nia knew how it felt to have a broken heart. In the past, she had cried so much that she reached the point that she couldn't cry anymore. Nia's sadness started to turn into bitterness, and in an effort to avoid another heartbreak, Nia did not go out with men. She focused on other things in her life, like being with her son, going to college, having a job, and being involved in church.

A lot of men asked Nia out, but Nia turned them down. Nia wanted to be alone and focus on her own goals in life.

Chapter #25

Asia noticed that Nia had not been out with a man for almost a year, and she felt that it was time for her friend to start going out on dates. Although quite a few decent men continued to asked Nia out, she continued to turn down every man that came her way. It's like Nia's afraid to get close to anyone again, thought Asia. She realized that Black had treated Nia very badly, but she couldn't help feeling that Nia was going to an extreme.

Asia could sense that Nia was lonely. Nia always tried to put on a front that she didn't need a man, but deep down inside Asia knew the truth. Nia was only twenty-five years old and Asia felt that she was too young to let life pass her by.

One day, Asia went to Nia's house to pay her a visit and to get her picture of her godson.

Nia and Asia sat down in Nia's dining room and talked over a cup of coffee. Devonte was out with Black for the weekend, so Nia was home alone. She missed not having her son around.

"So, Asia, how is your business doing?"

"Well, my clientele at the beauty shop is picking up. I believe that once I get some more clients and save up some more money, I will eventually open my own salon."

They talked about everything under the sun until their

conversation lead to the topic of dating and meeting someone special. Oh, Lord, not this subject again, thought Nia.

"Now Nia, I really do think you should start going out more."

"Asia, I do go out. I go to the movies sometimes."

"You mean with Devonte, or by yourself, or renting a movie! I don't consider that going out, Nia."

Nia sat there silently and listened to Asia.

"Nia, you need to go out with a man. Keith and I can see that you're lonely. Not all men are out to hurt you."

Asia looked across the table at Nia with deep concern and continued to talk.

"Nia, you're young and you should not let life pass you by. If you keep on turning down every man you meet, you just might miss Mr. Right."

What Asia told her made a lot of sense and had her really thinking.

"All right, Asia, I suppose you're right, I may consider going out sometimes. Now can we talk about something else, like your wedding?" asked Nia.

The topic of conversation moved on to other things, but this was not the last time that going out more was the main topic of conversation between the two of them.

Chapter 26

The gentle warm breeze of Southern California felt good against Nia's skin. It was now May 1995 and it was the beginning of spring. Asia and Nia were on their lunch break. They were outside eating their lunch.

"So Nia, are you still coming to the beauty shop on Friday to let me fix your hair?" asked Asia.

"Yeah I'm going to be there. This time I want to have my hair in a different style." answered Nia.

Asia thought of a perfect new hair style for Nia. "I know exactly what kind of style that would look great on you."

Nia looked at Asia's new hair style; her hair was so pretty. Asia had her hair dyed jet black and styled short just like the famous singer, Toni Braxton.

"Asia I love your hair it looks just like Toni Braxton's hair style."

"You do?" asked Asia with a smile.

"Yeah I do, who did it for you?"

"Oh Janis did my hair, the one who works with me at the beauty shop."

"Really? Tell her that she did a good job with your hair," said Nia.

"I will," respond Asia.

Nia thought that Asia's hair style fitted her face; it brought out her pretty slanted brown eyes and high cheekbones.

Nia had often wondered how Asia met Keith and how she knew that he was the right one for her so she asked.

"Asia, how did you meet Keith?"

"Well, to cut a long story short, I first met Keith when he was the assistant manager at Pizza Hut. Whenever I came into the restaurant, he used to always rush to take my order and offer me a free drink. At first, I thought he was just being friendly. I didn't have a clue that he was interested in me until one day he decided to ask me out."

"When he first asked you out, did you go out with him?" asked Nia, sipping on her soda.

"No, as a matter of fact I turned him down several times."

"Why wouldn't you go out with Keith?" She was shocked that Asia wasn't interested in Keith when she first met him.

"I didn't want to go out with him at first because I was still heart broken over Todd. I was afraid to get involved with another man. And, plus, I simply thought Keith was not my type because he's totally opposite of what I used to look for in a man. Usually I like tall dark-skinned men, but Keith was short and brown skinned. You know that Keith is only five feet, seven inches tall, but his heart is bigger than men twice his size. I love my baby." Asia enjoyed talking about her special relationship with Keith.

"How did you know that Keith was the right one for you?"

"Well at first I didn't know, because I wouldn't give the poor guy the time of day, and Keith will definitely tell you that for sure. But once I went out with him on that very first date, I just knew in my heart that he was the one for me," replied Asia.

"Oh, that's so sweet. I wish that I would meet someone special like you did," uttered Nia as she ate another french fry.

"Nia, you will meet a good man but you have to give someone a chance."

"You know what, Asia? You're right. I can't keep on holding on to my past, I need to move on with life. I guess I'm going to have to take another chance with another man and pray that he's Mr. Right. I know that God is going to bless me with a wonderful man that I'm going to marry someday."

"Great Nia! I'm glad that you're finally coming around. Maybe Keith can hook you up with one of his friends," suggested Asia.

"Well I don't know about that," Nia said hesitantly.

"Aw, come on, Nia! All you're doing is going out and having a nice time," said Asia, trying to convince Nia.

"OK, then I guess it wouldn't hurt, I suppose."

"Great, I'll ask Keith about some of his friends and see what he says."

"OK, then."

Later on that evening, Asia went over to Keith's house to have a nice quiet romantic dinner. Keith had cooked spaghetti with meat sauce and mushrooms, served with home made garlic bread and tossed salad. Along with dinner, they had red wine. Asia was enjoying dinner; she loved it when Keith planned romantic evenings for just the two of them. Keith was a wonderful cook and, he often cooked dinner for Asia.

Keith and Asia both had busy schedules. Keith worked full time as the general manager of Pizza Hut and also went to law school at night. Asia worked full-time at the dental office, part-time at the beauty shop, and was also busy trying to get her salon business off the ground. With such tight schedules, they still managed to see each other and spend quality time together.

After eating dinner, they put their dishes in the sink. Keith washed the dishes while Asia dried them and put them away.

"Keith, do you know if you have any nice available male friends that Nia could meet?"

Keith instantly thought about his main man Jabarie.

"Yeah, I know someone who would be good for Nia. As a matter of fact, I will see him at work tomorrow. I'll ask him if he would be interested in a hook up."

The next day finally arrived. While at work, Keith and Jabarie had a casual conversation. Jabarie was the assistant manager at the restaurant and he was the one that he wanted to set Nia up with on the blind date.

Their conversation began with sports and then it moved on to women and relationships.

"Man, speaking of women, I was wondering if you would be interested in going on a blind date," said Keith.

"Well, Keith, I'm going to have to think about this. You know that I already had one bad experience," Jabarie grimaced.

Jabarie was talking about a dreadful experience he had two weeks ago. His cousin Eric, had set him up on a horrible blind date with this fat unattractive woman, name Rhonda. Not only was Rhonda ugly, she also had the nerve to be stuck up and arrogant at the same time. Eric told him that Rhonda was fine, brown skinned, and had long pretty hair. What Eric failed to mention was that home girl weighed well over 300 pounds!

"Yeah, you must be talking about that awful blind date you

had with the fat chic. Man, I wouldn't let Eric set me up with nobody! All he dates are fat ugly women straight up!" laughed Keith.

While working, Jabarie, and thought about his last serious relationship. Stacy had been the woman he loved and dated for two and a half years. During their relationship, Stacy mistreated Jabarie. No matter what he tried to do to make her happy, she was never content.

Throughout their relationship, Stacy cheated behind Jabarie's back with different men. She even used him for money. Jabarie always gave her money to get her hair and nails done, to buy jewelry, and to buy new clothes. While dating her, Jabarie even bought her a used Ford Probe so she would have a way to get to and from work. After he bought her the car, she complained and asked him why he didn't buy her a brand new car!

Even though he did an awful lot for Stacy, she still complained about him not having any money. It seemed like no matter what he did, he could never satisfy her in any way. Jabarie kept on trying to make their relationship work, until Stacy dumped him for another guy.

After the unsuccessful relationship with Stacy and two others, Jabarie began to lose faith in black women. He wondered if there was just one good sister out there; and if there was one, where in the hell was she and when would he ever have the chance to meet this special someone.

Later that afternoon, Jabarie made up his mind that he would give the blind date a try; He knew that he could trust Keith's judgment when it came to women.

Jabarie approached Keith and asked him a few questions about the woman Keith was going to hook him up with.

"So, what's her name?" asked Jabarie.

"Her name is Nia."

"Does she have a job?"

"Yeah, she's a dental hygienist just like Asia,"

Jabarie grinned; he was impressed.

"Man, is this Nia fine in all the right places, because you know that I love a woman with a nice body?"

"Yeah, man," answered Keith.

"How old is she?"

"She's 25 years old," answered Keith.

Jabarie thought that was a good age because he was 28 and that made him three years older than she was.

"Does she have a sweet personality?"

"Yeah," sighed Keith because Jabarie was starting to get on his nerves with all the questions.

It was almost the end of the day, and Keith was tired and irritable, so he cut him off.

"Look, man, I wouldn't hook you up with just anyone, especially not someone like Stacy. I've known Nia for quite a long time, and Nia is one of Asia's closest and dearest friends. She is a very sweet person, and I thought she would be a nice person for you to meet. Now do you want to meet her or not, because you are starting to irritate me with the questions. Will you just trust me on this one?" asked Keith.

"Sure, man, I will give it a try."

"OK, then, I know that you're just curious about her but I think you'll like her. She's a warm-hearted and lovable person," Keith added.

Based on what little Keith told him about her, Jabarie felt quite good about this Nia character. Now he would have to wait and see for himself.

Chapter 27

Nia, Jabarie, Asia and Keith went on a double date the following Saturday. Nia and Jabarie wanted Asia and Keith to go with them, just in case the date didn't work out.

Earlier that evening, Asia was over at Nia's apartment trying to help her decide what to wear.

Nia said, "I've narrowed my decision down to two outfits. Should I wear this purple spandex dress or should I wear my blue Guess jeans with my rose colored halter top?"

"Girl, you should wear your blue jeans," answered Asia as she pointed to the outfit.

"You don't want the brother thinking that you're desperate with that hoochie mama dress on. Besides, we're only going to the movies and out to eat," responded Asia while blowing her nails to dry.

Nia nodded her head in agreement.

"I guess you're right. It's no point in over dressing. I'll wear the jeans," said Nia.

At 7:30, Jabarie and Keith arrived at Nia's; they were right on time. Keith rung the doorbell and Asia answered it.

"Hello, Baby," said Keith as he eyed her up and down and gave her a hug. Damn, my baby is fine he thought. He knew exactly what they were going to do after the date. She look real sexy in those short tight Daisy Dukes, thought Keith.

"Asia, you're looking real fly tonight," complimented Keith encircling her in his arms.

Keith whispered into Asia's ear. Whatever he told her made her giggle.

"Asia, you know Jabarie, I think you two already met."

"Yes, I remember him from that afternoon I picked you up from work," Asia shooked his hand.

"Hi Asia, how are you doing?" Jabarie asked politely.

"Oh, I'm doing fine," answered Asia.

"Nia will be out in a second, she's still trying to get herself together," added Asia.

Jabarie looked around the apartment and noticed that Nia had very good taste in furniture. The apartment was clean and neat; this alone made a good impression on Jabarie. Looking around the living room, he spotted a picture of a beautiful woman on the mantlepiece. He walked to the mantlepiece and picked up the frame to take a better look. Jabarie was intrigued with the woman's beauty in the picture.

The woman was a light honey-colored complexion with soft flawless skin. Her brown almond shaped eyes glistened like jewels. She had a lovely smile with dimples in each cheek and long silky jet black hair.

"Keith, come here for a second," said Jabarie gesturing for him to come.

Jabarie showed him the picture.

"Is this Nia?" asked Jabarie. He was hoping it was her; she was very attractive to him.

"Yes, that's Nia," answered Keith.

All Jabarie could do was smile, because now he couldn't wait to meet her. About fifteen minutes passed and Asia was ready to go; she didn't want to miss the movie.

"Nia, are you coming? You need to hurry up or we'll miss seeing the movie!" called out Asia

"I'm coming!" yelled Nia applying her Fashion Fair lipstick.

Nia finally entered the living room. "Hi, everyone, sorry for keeping you all waiting," apologized Nia.

Asia approached Nia and introduced her to Jabarie. "Nia, this is Jabarie, and Jabarie, this is Nia."

Nia looked up at the tall gorgeous man and said, "Hi Jabarie, I'm pleased to meet you."

Jabarie smiled at her and gazed directly into her eyes.

"It's nice to meet you, too."

Damn, home girl looks ten times better in person than she did in the picture, thought Jabarie. That picture does no justice as to how lovely she looks in person, he thought.

Nia was breath taken at Jabarie's handsomeness. He looked better than she had imagined; he was more than she had anticipated. Jabarie was about six feet, one inches tall and had skin as rich and smooth as caramel. He had the most beautiful light brown eyes she had ever seen. Nia also noticed his cute mustache.

After the movies, they went for dinner. They went to Red Lobster. At the restaurant, Jabarie had a chance to take a real good look at Nia. Jabarie thought that she was very cute; she had pretty soft skin and a warm smile. He also noticed that she had a nice body. She was extremely petite in frame and was also short. He figured that she was about five feet, two inches tall, because she came up to his shoulder.

Sitting at the table, Jabarie couldn't help but notice her breasts; he could see her cleavage from across the table. Suddenly his mind drifted, and he started to wonder if she was wearing a bra; he had felt the softness of her breasts when she accidentally brushed up against him in the movie theater. He couldn't take his mind off how beautiful she was.

When she got up from the table to go to the rest room with Asia, Jabarie liked how her tight jeans fitted snug against her body; she had a nice round firm butt, he thought.

After Asia and Nia left the table, Keith asked Jabarie what he thought about Nia.

"How is it going? I can tell you like her," grinned Keith.

"Yeah, I do. The girl has it going on. This was indeed a perfect hook up, man," said Jabarie with a large grin on his face.

Chapter #28

It was sunny and breezy in San Diego; the day was beautiful and filled with tranquillity. It was June 10,1995, and it was Keith and Asia's wedding day.

Nia was one of Asia's bridesmaids, and Jabarie was Keith's best man. The wedding was lovely and elegant; the colors they chose was gold and black.

Asia wore a long white satin dress trimmed in elegant sequence. Her dress fitted her snuggly and showed off her hour glass figure. She also wore a beautiful pearl choker necklace and matching ear rings. Asia had her hair done the day before the wedding, and she also had her nails manicured. This time, Asia's hair was in a short style similar to Halle Berry's.

During the ceremony, Nia became teary-eyed; she was so happy to see her friends uniting in holy matrimony. The wedding took place at New Birth Baptist Church. Keith and Asia's minister, Pastor Anderson, performed the ceremony.

"Asia, do you promise to love and cherish this man...," asked Reverend Anderson as he stood before the couple with his gold and black bible in his hand.

"I do," answered Asia looking deeply into Keith's eyes and

and smiling.

Reverend Anderson turned toward Keith and addressed him, "Do you, Keith, promise to love and cherish this woman..."

"I do," answered Keith as he gazed into Asia's eyes and held her hands in his.

Nia looked at Jabarie; he stood directly across from her. He caught her staring at him, and Nia looked away and blushed. She was embarrassed that he had caught her looking at him. Later, she looked at him again, and this time he winked at her and smiled. Nia beamed. He looks so handsome in that tuxedo, she thought.

Nia looked at Asia and Keith; they were exchanging their gold bands and placing them upon each others ring finger.

The preacher continued the ceremony, saying, "...I now pronounce you husband and wife. You may kiss the bride."

Keith took Asia into his arms and they melted into an everlasting kiss.

"You are now formally Mr. and Mrs. Samuels," added Pastor Anderson.

After the wedding, Keith and Asia had a small reception at the church. They hired a professional photographer to take wedding pictures.

Asia later stood on the stairs to throw her flowers. All the single women gathered in the middle of the floor to try to catch the bouquet of flowers, except for Nia. Nia was at the punch bowl getting Devonte something to drink. She noticed that her son's bow tie was crooked, so she knelt down to adjust it for him.

After adjusting Devonte's tie, Nia stood back up. When she turned around, she saw the bouquet of flowers sailing through the air in her direction. Nia reached up and caught the flowers. Asia laughed and covered her mouth when she saw that Nia had caught them.

Asia approached Nia and said, "Well I guess you're going to be the next bride real soon."

"Nah! I don't think so. I believe that I'll be an old maid before I ever become a wife," laughed Nia.

"I don't think so, because I see that Jabarie has the hots for you. Ever since you got here, he hasn't taken his eyes off you," observed Asia.

Nia knew that Asia was right because when she looked across the crowded room, she noticed that he was staring at her. Nia reached over and took Devonte by his small chubby hand; they walked to a table to sit down and eat.

In the months following the wedding, Nia found herself liking Jabarie more and more. She loved hearing his voice and talking to him. Often, they would talk to each other for hours on the phone and Nia realized through their long interesting conversations that they had much in common.

Their relationship was blossoming into a strong friendship, and in the mist of it a bond was growing between the two of them. For some reason, she felt that Jabarie was special and different from any man she has ever met.

Is he the one for me? she wondered countless times. Nah, he's just a good friend, speculated Nia; this is the start to a beautiful friendship, why ruin it with love and powerful emotions? thought Nia, as she sat back and analyzed their friendship.

Chapter #29

Jabarie just graduated from college and received his master degree in engineering at San Diego University; he already had a bachelors degree in mathematics. Nia was so proud of him; he finally reached his ultimate dream. Jabarie already did several interns with different firms so he also had some experience under his belt.

Jabarie sent his applications to other states other than just California; he felt that he would be limiting himself if he did other wise.

It was now August 1995. Nia and Jabarie went out on several dates and was enjoying their close relationship as friends.

What Jabarie liked the most about Nia was that she liked him. Even though she drove a nice 1991 Toyota Corolla, she still went out with him in his old beat up 1986 Ford Escort. Most women he dated in the past refused to go out with him because they didn't like his car and was embarrassed to be seen in it. But Nia was one of the few who could care less about what kind of car he drove or how much money he had in the bank; he knew that she really liked him.

Jabarie knew that Nia cared about him a lot because she showed it in so many ways. Whenever he needed anything, she was always there for him. When he became ill about a month ago, Nia came over and fixed him some soup and gave him his medicine; Nia

Nia came over to his apartment often to check up on him and make sure he was OK.

Lately, Jabarie has been thinking of Nia as more than just a friend but as someone he would love to be closer and intimate with. He has only known Nia for four months but it seem like he knew her for a lifetime.

On Christmas of 1995, Nia and Jabarie went to two dinners. They were both invited to Keith and Asia's first Christmas dinner in their new home; Jabarie was invited to his family dinner at his mother's house in Oakland, California.

They went over Asia and Keith's house first because their dinner was on Christmas Eve. On Christmas, they went to Jabarie's mother's house for Christmas dinner.

Once they got settled in Jabarie's small escort, they headed to Oakland. It took five hours to get there. During their long drive, they had a chance to talk and enjoy each others company.

"Gosh Nia, I wish that we could have brought Devonte along with us. I mentioned him a lot to my mother. I know she was really looking forward to meeting him," said Jabarie while keeping his eyes on the road and steering the car.

"I miss him too, Jabarie. But I promised his father that he could see him for the Christmas holiday. It's just not the same without him," agreed Nia.

"Jabarie what is your family like?" curiously asked Nia as she turned in the car seat to look at Jabarie; he's so cute she thought.

"Oh they're very down to earth type of people. You'll like them a lot. They're very friendly," answered Jabarie as he glanced over at Nia.

Nia thought that his eyes were so pretty; the color of his eyes changed from light brown to green.

"Jabarie, did you know that your eyes changes colors?" observed Nia.

"Yeah, people always say that. They change mainly when I change moods or it's just the way the light hits them."

"I bet you always get compliments on how beautiful yours eyes are," said Nia as she looked at him and leaned back in her seat.

"Yes, I do get compliments from time to time," said Jabarie modestly.

"Nia, you're going to have to try some of my mom's home-made cheesecake. My mom can show nuf cook some good food!"

"Really."

"Yeah, you'll see when we get there."

Finally, they arrived at his mother's house. Once he pulled up into the driveway, his little nieces, nephews, and cousins all ran up to Jabarie and gave him a hug. Nia noticed that kids loved Jabarie. Even her son, Devonte, has already took a liking to him.

After they walked in the door, they were all greeted. Jabarie introduced Nia to his family; he knew that they were curious about his new friend. One of Jabarie's kid cousins came up to him and sat next to him on the sofa.

His cousin's name was Kenneth.

Kenneth looked at Jabarie and asked him, "Is that your girlfriend?"

Jabarie looked at Nia and she smiled because she heard what he asked him.

"No she's a close friend of mine," answered Jabarie.

"Well she's much prettier and finer than that other girl you brought over last year. Why don't you ask her to be your girlfriend? I like her!" Kenneth grinned, showing off his snaggletooth.

Nia was so shocked at how well spoken and mature the kid

acted; he sounded like he was much older than he was.

"Boy what are you talkin about. You're only seven years old. Now how do you know if she's fine or not?" questioned Jabarie as he playfully put Kenneth into a head lock and winked at Nia at the same time.

"Hey man let me go!" laughed Kenneth.

Jabarie finally let the kid go.

"I can just look at her and tell that she's fine in all the right places," replied little Kenneth as he acted as if he was eyeing Nia up and down.

Kenneth was a cute little boy; he was brown skinned, skinny, with big brown eyes, and an ear ring in his left ear. Nia also met Kenneth's mom at the dinner; Nia could see why Kenneth behaved as he did. Kenneth's mom name was Shanequil.

Shanequil was a yellow women with bleached blond hair. She even wore a lot of gold jewelry, had a nose ring in her nose, and had on some long fake finger nails. Nia looked at what she had on and thought that it was sleazy; she had on a pair of Daisy Dukes shorts that almost show off the cheeks to her rear end and a see though blouse that showed off her black bra. Nia shook her head when she saw her; she felt that she didn't have no business dressing like that in front of her family and especially her son.

Jabarie later told Nia that Shanequil was a shake dancer at a strip club and Kenneth's father was in jail for armed robbery. Nia really felt sorry for Kenneth because he was growing up in almost the same environment she grew up in as a child. She hoped and prayed that his mom would get herself together. Nia felt that right now Kenneth needed his mother.

After eating dinner and socializing for a while, Jabarie and Nia finally left and went back home; they had a long journey ahead of them.

Finally they made it back to Nia's apartment at two O'clock in the morning. Both of them were exhausted.

"Guess what Nia?" asked Jabarie while closing the door.

"What?"

"My mom told me that she likes you."

"Really?" Nia smiled

"Yeah, and she also told me that she thought that you were a pretty young lady."

Nia blushed.

"Jabarie there's something I been wanting to tell you," said Nia as she looked away from the small decorated Christmas tree and over at him.

"What is it you wanted to tell me?" asked Jabarie while sitting comfortably on the soft sofa.

"I don't know if you feel the same way I do but my feelings for you is growing more and more each day. What I've been wanting to tell you is that I love you. I can't help it, it's just the way I feel. I would like it if we would eventually become more than just friends," softly said Nia as she looked at him and placed her hand over his.

What Nia told him sounded like music to his ears because he was feeling the same way too. The only reason why he never told her that he loved her was because he was afraid that she didn't feel the same way too.

"Nia, I love you too. I feel the same exact way you do. You are very special to me and yes, I do want us to be more than friends," said Jabarie as he looked into her eyes and ran his fingers through her hair.

Jabarie moved closer to Nia on the sofa and placed his arms around her waist. He leaned over and kissed her both lovingly and passionately on the lips. The kiss was tantalizing and Nia felt a burst of energy that ran down her spine. His strong hands gently caressed her arms and her shoulders; his touch felt so good against her skin.

They laid on the couch and enjoyed each other's embrace. Nia loved being in his strong arms. Through his shirt, she could feel the hardness of his muscles. Nia knew that she could really trust him.

Later, they exchanged their Christmas gifts. Nia bought Jabarie a brand new wallet; she noticed that he needed one badly. Several times, he had told her that he needed a new wallet. Jabarie was very happy and pleased with his gift Nia bought him.

Nia had a chance to open up her present. Jabarie bought Nia a porcelain unicorn to add to her collection. Nia thought that it the most precious gift that any man has ever given her. Nia leaned over and gave Jabarie a peck on the cheek to show that she loved her gift.

After that night, they moved up to a higher level in their relationship. They were not only friends but they were also lovers.

Chapter #30

Since Nia and Jabarie relationship has blossomed, Devonte and Jabarie started to have a strong relationship too. Jabarie really liked Devonte; he was a good child and was well behaved. Jabarie's relationship with Devonte had grown so much that he began to feel like Devonte was his own child.

Whenever Nia needed someone to pick up Devonte from day care, Jabarie would always come through for her. Nia could always rely on Jabarie because he was responsible and always kept his promises.

Jabarie did more for Devonte than Black ever did for his son. Black would much rather hang out with his friends rather than spend a little bit of time with his own son.

Often times, Nia loved watching Devonte and Jabarie doing things together. Jabarie was like the father that Devonte never had. Lately, Nia has also noticed that Devonte had been calling Jabarie daddy because he was always there for him.

When Jabarie and Nia first heard Devonte call him daddy they were both shocked.

Nia asked, "Who are you calling daddy?"

Devonte pointed his small index finger at Jabarie and smiled. Both Jabarie and Nia looked at each other in disbelief; they didn't know that Devonte associated Jabarie as being his father. And ever since that day, Devonte called Jabarie daddy since he was two and half years old.

Jabarie took Devonte to several places such as amusement parks,the circus, the zoo, and to the movies. Whenever they came back from their outings, Devonte would come back and tell Nia all about the wonderful things they did. Devonte spoke very well for his age and was already very talkative.

Whatever Devonte needed, Jabarie was always willing to get it for him.

One day, Black came to Nia's apartment to visit his son. While Black was sitting on the carpet playing with Devonte with his toys, the door bell rung.

Nia was in the kitchen so Black answered the door since he was the closest to the door. Black opened the door and saw this light skinned guy at the door.

"Hi, Is Nia here?" asked Jabarie.

"Yeah she's in the kitchen and who are you?" asked Black with sarcasm in his voice.

Black looked at him in a mean manner; he didn't like seeing this pretty boy nigga coming over to Nia's apartment.

"I'm her boyfriend, Jabarie."

Once Devonte heard Jabarie's voice, he got up from playing with his toys and ran towards Jabarie yelling, "Daddy, daddy, daddy!"

Jabarie smiled as he saw Devonte running his way. Once he reached Jabarie, he picked Devonte up in his arms and gave him a hug.

"How is it going little man," said Jabarie as he held Devonte and looked at him. "Fine, Daddy, are we going to McDonalds?" asked Devonte as he spoke to Jabarie.

"Yeah we might go if it's all right with your mother," answered

Jabarie.

Nia walked into the living room.

"Hi baby, I thought I heard your voice," said Nia as she went to the door way and gave Jabarie a kiss on the lips.

Black was furious and he felt completely left out. He couldn't believe that his own son of flesh and blood would be calling some other nigga daddy!

"Jabarie, you can come on in," said Nia.

"OK," said Jabarie.

"Black, this is Jabarie, Jabarie this is my ex, Black. He's Devonte's father."

"Please to meet you," said Jabarie as he reached out to shake Black's hand.

Black looked at Jabarie as if he was crazy; he didn't even bother to shake his hand. Instead Black grabbed Nia's arm and said, "We need to talk now!"

"OK." Black pulled Nia into the bedroom and started to fuss.

"Who in the hell is this nigga, Jabarie, and what in the fuck is my son doing calling this man daddy when I'm his real father!" roared Black.

"Well Black, Devonte hardly sees you because you never really be there for him. Ouch, Black you're hurting my arm!"

Jabarie could hear the argument from the other room so he put Devonte down to see what was going on. Jabarie stood at the door for for a split second. It enraged him when he saw Black violently shaking her and hollering at her.

"I'm going to do more than hurt you if don't answer me!"

"Let her go!" order Jabarie. Black looks up and see Jabarie standing in the doorway. Black finally lets her go.

"Nia, you know that is a lousy fuckin excuse!" yelled Black.

"Now look Black, you're not going to yell and curse me out in my own house! I asked and begged you countless times to pick up Devonte from day care and to spend more time with him since the day he was born and you chose not to, so don't you dare try to blame all this mess on me! I found a good man who loves both me and Devonte and is willing to be a real father to Devonte!" yelled Nia.

Jabarie watched for a brief second before he walked into the room.

"I think that it is time for you to be leaving! And I better not see you lay another hand on her again, or else I'll be kicking your ass!" yelled Jabarie, locking his cool eyes onto Black's and balling up his large fists.

"Hey, this is none of your business, man!" snapped Black.

"Well, it becomes my business when you're harassing my woman! Now it's time for you to be leaving!" ordered Jabarie.

"You haven't heard the last of this Nia, because what you did was straight out fuckin wrong and you're going to regret this. Devonte is my son and I'm going to fight to make it stay that way!" roared Black as he glared into her eyes and pointed his finger in her face.

Black stormed out of her apartment and slammed the door as he left.

Chapter #31

On February 1996, Nia received a letter in the mail from Black's attorney. Black was taking Nia to court to try to get custody over Devonte.

Once Nia saw and read the letter, she became devastated. Damn it Black how come you always like to hurt me thought Nia. Nia sat there for a moment and thought about what she should do about this situation.

Why does Black want our son she wondered. Nia knew that Black would be a sorry father; he rarely spent time with their son now, she thought.

What scared Nia the most was having Black take her son away from her. Nia knew how violent Black could get at times and she felt that if he ever got angry, he would only take all of his anger out on their son.

"I'm going to fight you on this one Black, because you're not going to take my son from me!" thought Nia aloud.

Nia didn't want her son to be raised in a violent home like she did when she was a child. She was determined not to let this happen to Devonte.

That evening, after Nia, Jabarie, and Devonte came back from the movies, Nia put Devonte to bed and read him a bed time story.

Once Devonte went to sleep, Nia went into the living room. Jabarie was sitting on the couch watching T.V. He turned off the television when Nia walked in.

"Is he sleep?" asked Jabarie.

"Yes, he is, he must have been real tired," said Nia.

"Yeah, little man did have a long day," agreed Jabarie as he looked at Nia.

"Nia, are you OK? It seems like something has been on your mind all day. Is there something you need to talk about?" questioned Jabarie.

"Yes I do have a lot on my mind. Gosh you know me so well, Jabarie. How did you know that?"

"I can tell by your facial expression and plus you been very quiet and to yourself all day. Come here, let me give you a massage to make you feel better."

Nia turned around to let him massage her shoulders. Jabarie started to massage her shoulders with his strong hands. His massage felt so good that she closed her eyes.   "Nia, you're so tense, just try to relax your muscles," whispered Jabarie. Nia finally relaxed her tensed muscles and began to feel much better.

"So baby are you going to tell me what's bothering you?" asked Jabarie while rubbing her shoulders.

"Jabarie, I received this letter from Black's lawyer," replied Nia.

"Why would Black's lawyer send you a letter through the mail?" curiously asked Jabarie.

"He's trying to take Devonte away form me! He's taking me to court to try to get custody over Devonte!"

"Why does he want custody over Devonte, he doesn't even spend time or money on his son," stated Jabarie.

"He's just doing this to hurt me. He thinks that since he makes more money than me and got his business off the ground that he can easily take Devonte away from me," said Nia sadly.

"Well Nia, I'm sorry that you're going through so much turmoil and I'm going to be by your side no matter what. My sister knows this lawyer who helped her during her custody battle with her ex-husband."

"Is this lawyer any good?" asked Nia.

"Yeah, he helped her win the case and she got full custody over her child. Her ex-husband had to pay both alimony and child support. I'll give her a call later to get the lawyer's phone number for you."

"Oh Thanks Jabarie, now I feel much better," said Nia as she kissed him on the cheek and then gave him a hug.

Meanwhile, Jabarie felt that they had a good relationship; but there were times when Jabarie could sense that Nia was holding a deep dark secret about her past. Often times, Jabarie noticed some scars on her body, such as the big burnt mark that he saw on her arm and the deep scar on her fore head. When ever he mentioned anything about those scars, she would always say that she was just clumsy and always want to get off the subject. He found it hard to believe her explanation because she acted very nervous.

Sometimes when he raised his voice when he's angry or even raise his hands when he's playing wrestling games with her, Nia would jump back from him and he could literally see the fear in her eyes. Jabarie some how had the feeling that she was afraid that he might hit her. He loved Nia and knew that he wouldn't do anything to hurt her. Jabarie wondered if Nia was a battered woman because that would explain why she seem scared of Black when ever he came over to visit

Devonte.

Eventually, Jabarie finally got Nia to tell him the truth. Nia told him about the abusive relationship she had with Black. Jabarie felt a whole lot better when Nia told him about her deep dark secret. Her honesty was what made them become even closer.

After she told him the truth, Jabarie gently kissed Nia's scar on her fore head and held her very close in a strong warm embrace.

He looked into her eyes and said, "Nia, I would never hit you. I couldn't ever imagine inflicting pain on someone I love so much."

Jabarie continued by saying, "I love you and I know that it's probably hard for you to completely trust another man again. I promise you, baby, that you don't have to worry about me hurting you. I'm here to love and to protect you. I want you to feel safe and secure with me."

Chapter 32

On Monday, April 22, 1996, Nia went to court. Before they went to court, John Wesley asked Nia various questions about her past relationship with Black and how he treated their son.

When Nia told him that Black used to beat her, he placed his reading glasses on the tip of his nose and continued puffing on his pipe; he began to ask more questions about the abuse.

"Ms. Chevez, do you have proof that he used to hit you?"

"Yes, my doctor took pictures of my bruises and scars."

"Have any of your friends seen these bruises?"

"Yes, my friend Asia has seen them."

"Do you know if Derrick (Black) cheated on you while you were together?"

"Yes, he did."

"Do you know how many times?"

"No... I don't know. Why are you asking me all of these questions?" Nia responded with irritation.

She didn't like him asking such personal questions. Answering questions about her past really made her uncomfortable.

"You need to be able to handle answering this type of question, because Mr. Carter's lawyers will be throwing questions like these in your face, so you'll have to get used to it. I need as much information as possible, so I can have my facts straight when we get in the court room. Ms. Chevez, the only way we're going to win this is if we have strong facts and hard core evidence to back us up."

Now, I have more questions to ask you, Ms. Chevez, so will you please answer them?"

Nia nodded her head in assent.

"OK, now. Does Black spend much time with Devonte?"

"No, he only comes to visit him once every other month."

"Has he ever threatened your son?"

"Yes, one time and that was when I decided to leave him. I didn't want him to hurt our son, too." Nia wiped tears from her eyes with a Kleenex.

After asking more countless questions, the lawyer told Nia that they had a strong chance of winning the case because they had so many negative facts and evidence proving that Black was an unfit parent.

The trial lasted for less than a week. The judge granted Nia custody of Devonte. Black stormed out of the court room in rage.

Nia was greatly relieved that the court case was finally closed. Nia, Jabarie, and Devonte went out that evening to celebrate their victory.

It was July of 1996, and the weather was very hot in California; the temperature was 98 degrees outside.

Nia and Jabarie had been dating for six months. Lately, Jabarie's sexual desires for Nia were growing greater and greater with each day.

Whenever he spent the night at her apartment or she spent the night at his place, they slept in the same bed, and he never made a move on her . Nia was very special to him, and he didn't want to pressure her into anything she wasn't ready for, but in his heart he felt that it was time to take the next step in their relationship. He wanted badly to make deep passionate love to her.

One hot summer day in July, Jabarie went over to Nia's apartment to visit her. Devonte was at the nursery, and Nia had taken a day off form work.

She met Jabarie at the door in a pair of snug blue jeans shorts and a haulter top. He knew that she was not wearing a bra, because he could see the imprint of her nipples throught her shirt; perspiration along her neck and face made her very sexy to him; and he could image how sweet she would taste against his tongue as he kissed every inch of her body. Jabarie noticed her tight stomach and cute little belly button. He looked down and saw that she was bare footed, and her feet were the smallest, cutest, most adorable feet he had ever seen. On her ankle she wore a beautiful gold bracelet.

"I'm glad that you decided to come by. What do you have planned for us today?" asked Nia.

"Well, I guess we can hang over here at your crib for a while; we don't spend enough quality time alone," responded Jabarie as he walked on in and eyed her up and down.

"Well, I guess I better warn you that my air conditioner is not working. Our landlord still hasn't fixed it yet," added Nia as she closed the door behind him.

Dang, he's so fine! thought Nia. Jabarie had on a pair of brown Timberlands and baggy fiting jeans. His hair was freshly cut into a low fade. She enjoyed running her fingers through his short hair, so soft to the touch that it reminded her of cottom. She loved the red Nike tank top he had on because it showed off his tight biceps. He also had on a Starters cap, but he took it off as soon as he came into her apartment.

"You mean to tell me that Mr. Jones has not fixed your air conditioner yet!" Jabarie sat down on the sofa.

"No, he hasn't sent a repairman yet." Nia walked towards Jabarie.

"Man, I don't see how you and Devonte can stand all of this heat. You all should come and stay at my place until they fix it."

"Word! That's why I'm dressed this way. I'm going to have to take you up on that offer, Jabarie."

Suddenly things got very quiet beween them. They made eye contact, and a wave of desire came over them. Jabarie got up and walked towards Nia, tilted his head and kissed her gently on the lips as he placed his powerful arms around her tiny waist. Nia gazed up at him speechless after the passionate kiss.

"Nia, you're very sexy and so desirable to me," said Jabarie in a deep, sexy tone of voice. He began to lead sweet trails of kisses along Nia's neck, and his hand moved from her waist on down to her soft round butt.

Nia closed her eyes and smiled fully savoring the tender moment. She felt an electric vibe along her body; she was very hot dure to the fiery flames of passion. That very moment Nia knew that she wanted Jabarie to make wild passsionate love to her.

She began to get wet between her legs, and her nipples started to harden. Jabarie's hands moved underneath her shirt. Nia loved the gentle touch of his hands as he caressed her bare breasts; her heart began to beat faster.

Jabarie engulfed Nia in his strong arms as he picked her up and carried her to the bedroom. Nia rubbed his huge mountain of biceps, feeling the hardness of his muscles. Touching his strong body thrilled her and made her want him inside of her even more.

Once he carried her to the bedroom, he laid her gently on the bed. Jabarie continued to kiss her as he took off her shirt. When he saw her lovely bare breasts, he moaned in lust and began to lick and suck them.

When Nia lay nude before him, she started to undress Jabarie. She took off his tank top and unbottoned the the buttons to his jeans. Later, he stood before her nude. His mighty chest was filled with manly soft curly hair and his bronze colored skin was rich and smooth. Nia could not take her eyes off his handsome body.

Jabarie sat back down on the bed and gently caressed Nia. For a moment, he stared at her beautiful body, loving the touch of her soft skin. He became fully erect just by looking at her . They stared into each other's eyes and held each other's hand in love. They merged together and made deep passionate longed-for love.

Chapter #33

In late August, Jabarie received a reply from one of the corporations he had contacted. Jabarie quickly opened up the letter and read it. The position that he had applied and interviewed for was available only in Atlanta. If he wanted the job he must move to Atlanta.

Jabarie was both happy and sad at the same time. He was happy because the job paid good money and sad because he would have to leave Nia and Devonte. He had hoped that the job would be somewhere in California.

Although Jabarie had five job offers in California, the job that he was most interested in was the one in Atlanta. The name of the coporation was Tech World Enterprises. Jabarie heard a lot of great things about Atlanta and he thought that it would be a nice city to live in.

Later that evening, Jabarie spoke to Nia about it over dinner. Nia told him that she thought that he should take the job because it was something that he always dreamed of doing, which was becoming an electrical engineer. She didn't want to interfere with his dreams.

The next day, Jabarie called Tech World Enterprise to accept the job. About a month later, in September, he was on a plane to Atlanta.

Both Nia and Devonte were in tears as they watched his plane take off into the sky. Little did they know that Jabarie was in tears too; he knew that he was going to truly miss them.

Chapter #34

It had been two months since Jabarie left California, and almost every day, Devonte asked Nia when his daddy was coming home. Nia knew that Devonte was taking Jabarie's absence very hard.

Jabarie called them twice a week to see how they were doing, but a telephone call was not nearly the same as actually having Jabarie with them. Nia missed Jabarie in many ways, she missed talking to him each night, going to sleep next to him, and making love.

Meanwhile in Atlanta, Jabarie was feeling the pain of missing both Nia and Devonte. Every night before he went bed, he would look at the picture they took as a family just before he left California.

Jabarie felt like Devonte was his own son. He loved spending time with him and doing things that a father would do with his son, things like playing baseball together and going fishing.

Not a day went by that he didn't think about Nia. She was such a beautiful woman to him both inside and out. Jabarie felt that Nia was a great person and that any man who had her in his life would be very lucky; Jabarie knew that he had a good woman, and he wanted badly to keep her.

At twenty-nine, Jabarie felt as if it were time for him to settle down and get married. Deep down in his heart, he felt that Nia was the right woman for him. She had been there for him when he didn't have anything, and she still loved him to this very day.

Jabarie decided that he was going to propose to Nia. Right after he got off work, he went straight to the jewelry store and bought Nia an engagement ring. He wanted to give her a special ring that would show how much he loved and cared for her.

Jabarie went to three different jewelry stores to find just the right ring for Nia. Finally, in a shop window, a ring caught his eyes. He smiled when he spotted it because he knew in his heart that this was the perfect ring. Jabarie went into the shop and purchased the ring.

Later that night, Jabarie called Nia on the phone. The phone rung twice, and Nia picked it up.

"Hello."

"Hi, Baby, how are you doing?"

"Oh, Jabarie, I'm doing fine. I miss you."

"I miss you too Baby. How is Devonte?"

"He's fine. I can tell he misses you too."

"Well, tell little man that I just bought you all some plane tickets to Atlanta."

"You did what!" exclaimed Nia in shock.

"I bought you all some plane tickets so you can come visit me here in Atlanta."

"Oh, Jabarie, that's wonderful! When can we come?"

"Can you leave in two weeks and take about two days off from work?" asked Jabarie.

"Yeah, I believe I can work that out."

"Well then, great! I'll have it set up so that you all can leave on Wednesday evening and be back on Sunday morning."

"OK."

"Well, Nia, I'm going to go to bed now. It's late, plus I have to finish these annual reports. Tell little man hello and that I love him."

"I will," said Nia.

"And Baby, just remember that I love you, I always have, and I always will," added Jabarie.

"And I love you, too, Jabarie."

"I'll see you and talk to you later."

"Good night, Jabarie."

"Good night, Nia."

Nia hugged herself tightly; she was so excited that she was going to see Jabarie soon. She couldn't wait to tell Devonte the news. She knew that he was going to be thrilled.

In November, Nia and Devonte flew to Atlanta. Nia was really looking forward to going to Atlanta, because she had never been there before. Devonte was so excited; he kept on peeking out of the window and asking his mom if they were there yet.

Finally, they landed at Atlanta's Hartsfield Airport. While they were picking up their luggage, Nia and Devonte spotted Jabarie. Jabarie drove them over to his town house in Riverdale. Nia and Devonte were so exhausted that they both went to sleep once he got them home.

The next day, Jabarie took them to different parts of Atlanta. He took them to Underground Atlanta, to the Coca Cola Factory, to the movies, and then out to eat.

Later that evening after Devonte went to sleep, Nia and Jabarie finally had some quiet time alone. Jabarie took Nia by the hand, and they went out to his sun porch.

"It's so beautiful outside," murmured Nia.

"It is," agreed Jabarie, and he looked at Nia and watched her eyes glitter with joy.

"Look, the stars are so bright! Look over there at the brightest star in the sky. I wonder if that's the North Star?" Nia pointed her index finger towards the sky.

"It might be. I'm not an astronomer, so I don't really know," said Jabarie as he stood behind Nia and wrapped his arms around her in a strong embrace.

"Jabarie, I want you to know how much I love and appreciate you. You're really a good man. You came into our lives and loved and treated us so right. I have to admit that you're very special, because not too many brothers would accept a boy as their son, if he's not their own," expressed Nia.

Nia turned around and looked up into Jabarie's hazel brown eyes.

"Jabarie, I love you so much, and you're so special to me."

"And, Nia, you're special to me, and I love you, too. Not being with you for more than two months has shown me how much you all really mean to me. You two are my family." Jabarie gently caressed her soft cheeks.

"Nia, there's something that I've been wanting to ask you." Jabarie got down on his knees and pulled out a small black box from his pocket.

"Will you marry me?" asked Jabarie opening the box and showing her the stunning diamond ring.

"I would love to marry you," whispered Nia with tears of joy in her eyes.

Jabarie stood back up and placed the ring on her finger. he leaned over and kissed her on the lips.

"It's so beautiful," said Nia as she admired the ring.

"It's beautiful just like you," said Jabarie as he watched her. He gently swept a strain of her long dark hair away from her face.

"Nia, now we are going to be officially united as a family."

Nia cried because what he said really touched her heart.

"Why are you crying, Baby?"

"I'm crying because I'm so happy, this is what I always dreamed of having a family to call my own that truly loves me."

"Well, I guess your dream has now become a reality." Jabarie continued to hold her in his arms.

They both looked up at the clear dark sky and admired the twinkling stars. They looked forward to a bright future with love and unity. They both knew that the love they felt for each other was definitely a blessing from God.

Bibliography

Kimberly S. Phillips is an Atlanta native. Currently the author resides in Atlanta, Georgia with her husband and daughter. Coming soon is her next novel *A Dancer's Dream*.

If you enjoyed and loved the character, Nia, look forward to the spin off from *Purpose Lies Within*; the spin off novel is *Silhouette's Luv*. Kimberly Phillips wants to hear from you! You can email her at: kphilli4@bellsouth.net!

Purpose Lies Within
By: Kimberly S. Phillips
"Nia" mean purpose in Swahili
and is one of the principles practiced in
Kwanzaa. Nia finds her purpose in life
which is to fall in love!
Send *Purpose Lies Within to a*
friend, a perfect gift for Kwanzaa,
Christmas, or any time of the year. Here's
how to order:
ISBN#0-9667913-0-4/$15.95

Payable in U.S. funds. No cash orders accepted.
Postage and Handling: $1.75
for one book, $.75 for each additional. Maximum
postage $5.50. Prices,
postage, and handling charges may change at any
time. (Purpose Lies Within)

Send this order form to: Bill my: VISA___
    Messenger Publishing   MASTER___
    P.O. Box 373424   AMEX___
    Decatur, GA 30037   DISCOVER___
Card #_____
Signature_____
or call 1-(877)323-6622 to order   or enclosed is my:
        ___Check ___Money Order
        (Make checks and money order out to
        Messenger Publishing)
        *Please allow 6 weeks for delivery
        Name:_____
        Address:_____
        City/State:_____
        Zip:_____
        Book Total: $_____
        Postage and Handling: $_____
        Sales Tax: $_____
        Total Amount Due: $_____